BOOKS IN THIS SERIES OF KNIGHTS

AUTHOR JOHN F. TUSKIN.

POWERFUL KNIGHT IN BLACK
Story of Knights

JOHN F. TUSKIN

authorHOUSE®

AuthorHouse™ UK Ltd.
1663 Liberty Drive
Bloomington, IN 47403 USA
www.authorhouse.co.uk
Phone: 0800.197.4150

Published by AuthorHouse   04/28/2014

ISBN: 978-1-4969-7910-0 (sc)
ISBN: 978-1-4969-7911-7 (hc)
ISBN: 978-1-4969-7912-4 (e)

Contents

Chapter One

Alibi

The screams from his mother were a regular occurrence for the fourteen year old boy named Gettard, he again watched with horror as his father beat his mother with a belt.

His father Lord Dayton Endevoure is a large brute of a man with an oversized belly from all his heavy drinking that he had achieved from all the years of being the keeper of the keys at the dungeons in the castle of Tonest.

Having just returned home in the evening from his daily drinking binge, he was now, at this moment in time, taking out his frustrations from his job on his wife after she had again said something that he had taken offence to.

This Lords unfortunate wife is Lady Helena Endevoure, the Kings younger sister.

Being a very close friend and protector to the King, Lord Endevoure with his family are privileged enough to be living in their chambers at this castle of Tonest.

To Gettard this day was not different in any way from any other day but something just clicked within the brain of this young boy. Being very tall with strong striking features, his short jet black hair matched the blackness of his eyes, his body being thick set was any match for other boys of his own age. With his fists now clenched tightly he suddenly lunged at speed towards his father's oversized torso.

"Leave her alone you coward."

Shouted Gettard as his fists connected with several punches to the head of his father sending him sprawling to the ground with such force that his father hit the back of his head on the stone floor knocking him unconscious.

"Gettard what have you done?" His mother cried, who at this time, with a lot of effort, finally managed to lift her battered body from off the floor.

Now standing unsteadily on her feet Lady Helena who was tall with a slender body had scars on her once pretty face from previous beatings that were also inflicted by her husband's buckle, her hair being black and long covered most of these imperfections.

She now feared for her son's future because of his intervention as she went on to say.

"Gettard you had better go and fetch Ordmin he will know what to do and how to sort this terrible mess out."

Ordmin, who at this time is the Kings personal adviser, and is also a very good friend of Lady Helena, Some people at the castle would say that he would have married Lady Helena if it had not been for political reasons that her brother the King demanded that she had to marry into a title, so the King had chosen Lord Endevoure as her husband.

Castle Tonest's King at this time was King Hagair Victinours a strong tyrant of a King who had achieved his Kingdom by defeating his enemies in lots of fierce battles showing little mercy towards any of his adversaries.

This King also has two sons. Drago who is eighteen is the eldest with Hobart his younger brother who is the same age as Gettard; "Fourteen." Having been brought up together as cousins Gettard and Hobart were forced to play in each other's company but were never friends whereas Drago being the oldest and heir to the throne was a law to his own, he would disappear on his horse from the castle for several days at a time without anyone knowing where or when he would appear again.

Looking very worried at what he had just done, Gettard raced along the long corridors of this castle towards Ordmin's quarters, after rapidly knocking on the main door of this adviser's suite of rooms, a medium sized well dressed good looking man with a beard that partly covered a scar down the left side of his face eventually appeared.

"Hello Gettard you look upset what can I do for you?" Ordmin uttered after being surprised that someone had actually knocked on his door because they hardly ever did in this castle of Tonest.

The words just seemed to blurt out of Gettard's mouth at an alarming speed as he replied. "I've killed my dad, I hit him, he is lying on the floor motionless, think he is dead. What shall I do?"

Knowing that Gettard's mother and father had always had their marital problems in these last few years at the castle, Ordmin answered while closing his door behind him as he made his way out into the corridor. "Now, now Gettard stop worrying, come on let's see what you have done and hope I can help you sort this problem out."

Arriving back at the scene of the attack Ordmin found Gettard's mother, Lady Helena actually standing over her husband's body with a blooded candle stick in her hand, on seeing Ordmin entering into her chambers Lady Helena cried out in panic, "It's not my fault he attacked me again, he should not have done that."

There sprawled awkwardly across the floor facing up in front of everyone with his eyes fixed staring to the chambers rafters along with his mouth wide open was Lord Dayton Endevoure lying there obviously dead covered in blood with a nasty deep gash on the front of his forehead.

Ordmin looking down at his oversized battered body said with a bit of sadistic humour. "If he was not dead before he surely is now with a hole like that in his skull you can almost see daylight from the back of his head. What have you done Helena? Your brother the King is not going to be that happy at losing his friend. We shall have to make it look like some sort of accident otherwise you will be sent to the gallows even though you are the King's sister, I know what our King is like he will make no exceptions even for you."

With his mouth open wide from the shock of seeing his mother standing there over his demised father's body, Gettard was suddenly startled out of his trance when Ordmin said to him. "Close your mouth boy and grab your father's legs while I hold on to his shoulders."

Lifting this corpse onto the large carpet that was laying as part of the furnishings in their chambers, Gettard with Ordmin rolled the carpet around the body as to conceal the evidence of Lady Helena's crime.

"Now Gettard help me place the body in the corner of the room." Ordmin said as he lifted his end of the carpet with a lot of effort from Lord Endevoure's dead weight.

It was as they were placing the body on the floor that there was an abrupt sharp knock on the outside of their chamber's door, this sudden noise made Lady Helena jump up an inch from the stone floor that she was standing on before saying. "Oh I forgot I expect that will be the new young medicine man called Cretorex who I told to call with some liniment for my husband's aches, what shall I do? Shall I tell him to go away?"

"No don't do that." Ordmin said. "Let him in, he could not have come at a better time, I have just thought of a plan where this man called Cretorex could help us."

As Lady Helena opened the door she still held on tightly to the blooded candle stick, that's when Gettard suddenly moved across the room from behind her with tremendous speed before snatching it out of her hand so that this visitor called Cretorex had no chance of seeing it.

Cretorex the new healer had only recently been allowed to treat most of the residents at this castle after their King had heard of his reputation as being the best healer of ailments in his realm of Tonest.

Standing there with his brown sack cloth bag of medicines over his shoulder, Cretorex a tall thin man with long black hair dressed in a long brown smock that reached down to his boots began to say to Lady Helena. "I have come to treat Lord Endevoure; may I come in my Lady?"

Stuttering slightly with her nerves uptight Lady Helena replied.

"I'm sorry but Lord Endevoure is not here, you can give me the liniment I shall treat him when he arrives home."

Before Cretorex had a chance to hand over the ointment to her Ladyship, Ordmin called out behind her from inside the room.

"Lady Helena you must let Cretorex in I need to talk to him?"

As Cretorex stepped into the room he thought Lady Helena was making excuses for her husband to be out because he mistook Ordmin as being Lord Endevoure when he said to him.

"I know you are busy my Lord but I will be as quick as I can in treating you, now where exactly on your body are you aching?"

The medicine man took Ordmin by surprise with this suggestion resulting in Ordmin almost choking with a cough as he replied sternly.

"No! I am not Lord Endevoure her ladyship is telling you the truth. My name is Ordmin the Kings personal adviser, I am here on the Kings business, but while you are here you can help me, I need some sort of potion or tonic for this severe headache that I have had these last few days, what would you suggest I should take that could ease it."

Apologising for his mistake Cretorex handed over a pouch of powder to Ordmin but not before warning him that too much of this powder at any one time would result in sending the consumer into a deep sleep for up to three to four hours, so Cretorex made sure that Ordmin was instructed in the right dosage that he should administer to himself. This was good news for Ordmin it was just the tonic he was wishing for to help him in his next scheme to clear up this mess of the unexpected demise of Lord Endevoure.

When Cretorex had left Lord Endevoure's chambers to carry on with his visits to see the rest of his patients within this castle, Ordmin instructed Lady Helena to prepare several jugs of mead with an added over-dosage of this headache potion for the castle guards that were positioned in several areas around the castle corridors in the direction of the dungeons.

When the drinks were prepared Ordmin told Gettard to place them on the back of a shield so that the young boy could carry these drinks to the castle guards as a gift along with the story that it was his father, Lord Endevoure's birthday.

As Gettard had placed the last of eight of these jugs on the shield he began to have an unnerving thought of what was about to happen so he decided to say to Ordmin,

"What if they know the date of my father's birthday?"

With his hand now in the middle of the young boys back Ordmin started to push firmly against Gettard edging him towards the door of the chambers while replying.

"That's a chance we shall have to take. Now make sure you also serve the two guards at the bottom of the steps inside the dungeons, also you will have to stay around to see if the drug has done its work. When all the guards are asleep come back here quickly to help me move your father's body. Now off you go and good luck."

Chapter Two

Lucky Escape

Walking along the long corridor Gettard's brain was working overtime wondering what Ordmin was planning to do with his father's body.

With his thoughts elsewhere Gettard was abruptly awakened from his dreaming by the voice of the first guard that he had suddenly come upon.

"Hello young man where are you going with that shield of jugs?"

Even though all the guards in the castle knew who Gettard was they would on the King's instructions still challenge any one who looked suspicious like holding a shield in this way.

Nervous of his task in hand Gettard replied hesitantly. "I have been instructed by my mother and father to supply a jug of mead to all the guards that protect these corridors also my father's guards at the dungeons, so that you can celebrate his birthday which happens to be today."

This first guard's face lit up at the thought of receiving a freebee as did the rest of the six guards that Gettard met on his way until he finally served the last two at the bottom of the steps in the dungeon.

All these guards guzzled their drinks as fast as they could as though it would be their last which made the potion within these drinks work a lot faster in knocking them out into a deep sleep.

With his task now completed Gettard retrieved the jugs from the now sleeping guards and quickly made his way back to his chambers where Ordmin with his mother were waiting patiently.

As soon as Gettard entered into the chambers, Ordmin with a lot of anxiety decided to ask. "Well young Gettard did it work, are they all asleep, can we now proceed to move your father's body?"

Gettard placed the shield of empty jugs down while replying. "Yes sir, they are all out for the count, now where are we taking my father?"

"All in good time, you will see when we get there. Now help me lift your father up again." Ordmin said, as he went over to lift up the heavy part of the carpet again. Lifting it with a lot of effort he went on to say to Lady Helena. "My lady, would you please open the door for us and see if the coast is clear outside."

With the corridor clear Ordmin, with Gettard, struggled, with the weight of Lord Endevoure's body, towards the dungeons.

When they arrived at the top of the steps at the dungeon entrance the guards were still fast asleep from their unexpected birthday treat.

It was there that Ordmin told Gettard to place his end of the carpet to the ground, on doing so Ordmin placed his end down at the same time. Then with a tug they both unrolled the carpet allowing the body of Lord Endevoure to roll down the stone steps and into the dungeons.

Even with the sight of his father's crumbled body at the bottom of these steps Gettard felt no emotion towards his father because of all those years of brutality that his father had used against himself and his mother.

Rolling up the carpet again Ordmin placed it into Gettard's arms before saying. "Let's hope that everybody thinks he has accidentally fallen to his death, we shall have to pray that no one finds out what really happened to your father. We should now go outside to the courtyard and clean the blood from this carpet at the castle well, before any of these guards awake."

Successful in their cleaning of the carpet; this young boy with his elder started their walk back along the long corridor only to come face to face with the Kings younger son, Hobart, who was at this time trying to wake up one of the sleeping guards by shaking this guard's shoulder profusely?

On seeing his cousin brought back bad memories of his past experiences in his life with this young Prince.

From these encounters Gettard had learned not to trust this young prince because he would on a regular basis report back to his father the King anything unusual that he had seen.

"Hello' what have you two been up to with that carpet you are carrying?"

The young Prince demanded as he thought the two of them were looking slightly furtive as they passed him in the long corridor.

Before either of them could answer a voice shouted from along the top end of the corridor, it was Lady Helena who had just happened to look out of her chamber's door to see if her son and Ordmin were on their way back. "There both of you are. What took you so long, did you manage to clean all that sick off the carpet for me?"

Ordmin shouted back in quick response.

"Yes we did my Lady the carpet is nice and clean now with no stain visible?"

"Oh, so that's what you have been doing, who's been sick? Was it you Gettard?" And by the way do you know anything about why this guard is fast asleep on duty?"

These prince's questions were blurted out in quick procession before Gettard had a chance to talk when Ordmin was just as quick when he answered these questions for him.

"No idea sir, the guard was fully awake when we passed him on our way to clean the carpet outside. The mess on the carpet was from Lord Endevoure's overindulgence in Mead again."

Then with a slight pause, Ordmin went on to say.

"I don't suppose you might have seen him somewhere because after he was embarrassed by being sick he disappeared down the corridor?"

Being satisfied with the excuse of the carpet Prince Hobart replied sharply.

"No I haven't seen him, but this guard will pay for being asleep on duty when I report back to my father."

Leaving Prince Hobart to sort the guard out Ordmin with Gettard arrived back at the chamber's of Lady Endevoure where they agreed they would all have the same story to tell for the next morning.

Ordmin was now satisfied he had covered all the problems for this night, so he decided they should all retire to their relevant beds in their chambers and wait for what the morning had to offer.

Peace was brought to the chamber's of the Endevoure's that night for the first time in many a year as her Ladyship retired to her cot in the knowledge of knowing she would not be battered again by her husband.

Also that night while sleeping Gettard had a pleasant vivid dream about himself in the future as a man in black armour riding on a large black horse while holding a lance and shield, displayed on the face of this shield was a flying bat along with a black plume protruding from the top of his helm.

Within this experience he encountered other knights that he had conquered in combat along with weird creatures floating above aimlessly in the skies in and around many of these battles.

When he awoke the next morning little did he know that the dreams he had that night would one day become a reality.

One thing he did know was he would never tell anyone of these dreams in case they would think that he was a fool.

Chapter Three

Free of Blame

Six years earlier when Gettard and Prince Hobart were eight was a time of turmoil when the castle had just been built by the King's stonemasons which had taken them almost ten years to build.

The castle was a square thick walled structure with four large turrets that dominated each corner, behind and upon these walls with their turrets' ramparts had been built for lookout posts against any assailants.

Built within a large clearing of Tonest forest the front elevation had no moat to its impressive draw bridge in front of its gates.

Inside this castle the spacious courtyard with its stables, armoury, and sleeping quarters for the guards with their parade area outside that led to the steps to the main building which consisted of the chambers for the King and his Lords with their Ladies.

Also within this building was the grand hall with its kitchens situated behind a door at the far end. Within this hall was a very long table where the King would command his men or use it for dining.

Near the entrance to the main building the dungeons were conveniently situated for the king's punishment area outside.

Before this castle was built, King Hagair, with his men and their families, would roam the lands as nomads pillaging and conquering other tribes until their power was so great that no other tribe or nation was powerful or large enough to fight back.

Through his leadership making sure his army of men were well supplied with wealth and food, Hagair, as he was known then, was made a King by his men at a time just after the first bricks were laid for his castle of Tonest.

From that day King Hagair had ruled with such a strict code of conduct that he was at most times feared by all.

That is why that night when the guards in the dungeon's had awakened from their drugged induced sleep to discover the body of Lord Endevoure at the bottom of the dungeon steps they had decided for fear of reprisal from their King was to take this body of Lord Endevoure out into the darkened courtyard then place it at the bottom of the rampart steps to make it look as though this Lord had fallen from the ramparts.

To fall asleep on guard duty was repaid by a public flogging of a hundred lashes laid bare from the edge of a willow bow which is what that unfortunate guard was about to receive that very next morning after that snitch Prince Hobart had reported back to his father the King.

It was the immediate decree from the King that sent the servants, guards and general personnel of the castle to gather for the flogging in the castle grounds, it was also then that the rat bitten semi-decomposed body of Lord Endevoure was discovered by the same crowd.

Being that Lord Endevoure was King Hagair's right hand man from the start of his conquests, the King decided to see for himself on how the unfortunate demise of his friend had happened.

Appearing on the scene with his personal guards around him, the King walked with a limp from a wound he had received from one of his many battles, he was six foot in size, slim and dressed in fine clothes, he had long black hair down to his shoulders and a protruding sharp nose with beady eyes that were covered by black bushy eyebrows.

Now looking down at the rotting corps the King decided to summon Ordmin his advisor to attend the scene.

With the immediate arrival of Ordmin who knew this King from his past experiences that he should never ever be kept waiting, stood cautiously in front of the King, bowed his head along with the words.

"Your royal highness, how can I help?"

The King upset from what he had seen, answered with a sharp sarcastic voice. "Help; How can you help; you idiot I want you to find out how this travesty has happened to my friend?"

Ordmin was used to the King's ravings from the first day he was appointed as the King's adviser, to him this was good news he could now keep up the pretence and fabrication on how Lord Endevoure had come to his demise.

"Yes sire" he said, "I shall look in to it straight away. May I beg your leave?"

The King nodded in response followed by a passing of his hand to send Ordmin on his way. Taking a last look at his friend laying there the King then ordered his guards to remove the body back to a room inside, then with his entourage in tow walked over to watch the commencement of the punishment being given to his disobedient guard.

Reporting back at the chambers of Lady Endevoure, Ordmin found the King's son, Prince Hobart at the door again interfering by his questions towards Gettard on what he was really doing the night before.

Prince Hobart was the King's second child therefore he would always try his hardest to please his father especially when his mother the late Queen had died giving birth to him, he had always felt his father had never forgiven him for his own birth.

Deciding enough is enough; Ordmin abruptly put the young Prince in his place by saying.

"Sir, whether you believe us or not you had your answer last night, take that as the truth and go back to your father, I believe he will need you with him at this moment in time."

"Hmph;" Was the reply as Hobart shrugged his shoulders, turned then despondently walked off down the corridor.

With the prince now out of the way Ordmin placed his hand on Gettard's arm as he gently pushed him back into the room where Lady Endevoure was hiding behind the door.

"You both have nothing to fear."

Ordmin said in a soft voice then went on to say.

"It looks as though the guards from the dungeons put the Lord's body outside last night at the bottom of the ramparts, now the King has left it to me to find out how Lord Endevoure met his death."

To Gettard and his mother a sigh of relief came over both of them that Ordmin had saved the day for them, he did not know it now, but in years to come this would not be the only time that Ordmin would be there to help him out of a problem.

After two days of covering his tracks with pretending to question observers as to when they had or had not seen Lord Endevoure on that fateful night, Ordmin reported back to his King with the story that the Kings friend had met his death after drinking too much, whilst climbing the steps to the ramparts in a drunken state had then slipped from them to his death.

Several days of mourning for Lady Endevoure and her son is all it took to convince her brother the King that there was no sinister act against his now deceased friend.

On the fourth day Lord Endevoure was cremated on a large pyre at a hill to the rear of the castle, most of the castle's inhabitants were ordered by the King to attend.

Chapter Four

The Annoying Man

At the time when the castle was built the majority of the king's soldiers with their families had settled in a make shift camp at a clearing to the other side of Tonest forest some several miles away called the garrison.

But over the years it had become a well established fortified fortress with walls that were ten foot high made from solid tree trunks. The two main gates centred directly within these walls were made of thick dense oak spanning approximately twelve feet across.

Inside this defensive barricade was a large settlement of houses mixed with dwellings for different types of trade which aligned the well trodden streets that eventually led towards a large central stoned manor house.

From the start of this settlement King Hagair had left one of his war lords to take charge of the running the day to day affairs of this fortress, his name was Lord Darnley a middle aged widower who had lost his wife some years previous to swamp fever but had brought up his only daughter, Silvianda, a beautiful shapely girl with long black hair that reached down to her waist.

Now at the age of fourteen Silvianda was a happy go lucky girl who loved to play outdoors with other youngsters of her age than having to stay indoors studying, most girls of her age were either betrothed or already married but Silvianda was far too fond of her father to go into a relationship for marriage.

King Hagair who realised the girl was at the right age would keep hinting to Lord Darnley to allow his oldest son Drago to visit Silvianda with the hope that they would become friends then from there on, one day, would eventually marry.

The only problem was Prince Drago was never around long enough in one place to allow this courtship to happen.

Lord Darnley a rugged man with a soft and a generous heart for his only daughter was just as kind hearted to most of the community in the garrison, he also knew Prince Drago was an unruly womaniser from various stories he had heard from travellers who happened to stop over at the garrison.

With this in mind Lord Darnley on many occasions with information that Prince Drago was about to visit his garrison would send his courier to the castle with an excuse to say his daughter was either ill or somewhere else so as to keep her safe from the hands of this Casanova Prince.

This courier's name was Vileri a weasel of a man who had a knack of creeping up to any authority that might happen to be around.

Short and lean in stature with long strait black hair down to his round hunchback shoulders, a small black beard with a thin pointed moustache, with eyes that sank well into his features above a short pointed nose that shadowed a thin wide mouth which always seemed when opened to find the right answer to any question that might be asked of him.

It was a week later after the death of Lord Dayton Endevoure that Vileri had just arrived at Tonest castle on one of his many visits as messenger for Lord Darnley.

Entering into the grand hall after being given an audience with the King; Vileri's small stature stood in front of the great table where Ordmin and several lords were sitting with his majesty.

Behind the King was his eldest son Prince Drago standing there in the finest of clothes while making a rare appearance on this day, this prince was six feet in height his hair long, red and wavy matched the colour of his skin on his handsome face which had been obtained through all his lazing about naked in the sun while flirting with other girls, his eyes the colour of electric blue under long ginger eye lashes complemented his perfectly formed nose over a strong square chin.

Looking sternly at the courier the King said. "Well what excuse have you brought me this time from 'Thunderblast'?" (This was a nickname the King always fondly used for Lord Darnley that went back in time to those early war years).

Vileri replied in his usual uncomfortable creepy crawly way.

"Your highest and most gracious majesty, His Lordship begs your forgiveness as my Lords only daughter the lovely Silvianda has unfortunately succumbed to chicken pox which has tarnished her soft and wonderful skin with the unsightly marks of blemishes in the shapes of spots and is at this moment in time unable to receive your revered and most handsomely strong son for escorting on this glorious day until her lady recovers' from her sickness."

Prince Drago sniggered from behind the King to the excuses of this irritating little man; to him he was not bothered he could have any young damsel out there that he happened to find.

The King responded to his son's silly noise.

"Silence boy?"

Then looking to Vileri he said.

"You can tell Lord Darnley I am not happy with all these excuses so I have now decided to send Lady Endevoure back with you to the garrison to keep a closer eye on this young daughter of his. You can stay here for the night then at first light tomorrow Lady Endevoure shall be ready for you to escort her back there."

Passing his hand through the air as he beckoned Vileri to go, the King went on to say. "You are now excused."

Vileri not missing a chance to have the last word replied.

"What a wonderful idea your highness; only a great King such as yourself could think of this most glorious of solutions."

King Hagar had now lost patience with this courier as he shouted. "Get out you idiot."

Vileri realised he had said too much backed off bowing as he fled his King's impatience.

With the irritating weasel out of the way King Hagair now discussed with his lords the future he had in store for the inhabitants of Tonest castle.

"I have decided that from now on all young men from the age of twelve will join a special training camp to learn the art of warfare in the hope that one day some of them shall become Knights. The person I have chosen to run this camp will be my personal adviser Ordmin."

Ordmin on hearing he had been chosen nearly slipped off his seat in shock.

"Ahm Thank you, your highness, I am honoured."

Ordmin said hesitantly while choking before the King quickly replied.

"Don't worry you shall earn every second of your time for me especially as your first students will be both my uncontrollable sons along with my young nephew Gettard."

This day for Ordmin would be a great turning point in his own life when there would be no looking back, his love for Lady Endevoure taken from him together with a change in his career as he was at this time the adviser to the King but would now be a trainer in warfare to young men.

Next morning at the chambers of the Endevoure family the maids and servants were helping with the removal of Lady Helena's goods and chattels. Gettard was also there helping his mother to pack her personal belongings for her arduous move to the garrison.

After the last of her maids with the servants had left struggling with her luggage to the outside after closing the door behind them, Lady Helena with tears in her eyes said her goodbyes to her son with some words of advice for her son's future.

"Be true to yourself never back down from a fight as long as you know you are on the side of good and it is of a just cause, most of all trust no one only take others on face value so tread carefully in your life my son?"

Gettard's eyes started to water while trying to hold back the tears when he replied.

"I will mother, I shall also, when possible, make it a point to visit you at the garrison to see that you are keeping well."

With her words of wisdom spoken Lady Endevoure cuddled her son for a last embrace before she started her departure with her personal maid, only to be interrupted from a knock on the outside of her chamber door.

The voice of Ordmin was heard from behind this door.

"Are you ready Lady Helena? That little courier Vileri has a carriage waiting for you outside in the castle court yard."

Opening the door Lady Endevoure had one more request for Ordmin before she left the castle.

"I am ready Ordmin, can I rely on you to look after my son and promise me to keep him out of harm's way?"

Ordmin; being an intelligent man replied.

"I will look after him as I shall look after all my future students that happen to come to me for tuition, but to keep him out of danger I cannot promise, that would be in the hands of fate and is part of your son's growing up to become "in my eyes!" one day a great Knight."

Helping Lady Helena with her maid down the long corridors with her personal belongings, Ordmin with Gettard finally opened the door at the top of the steps out into the court yard to find Vileri who was wearing a large red brimmed hat bearing a colourful peacock feather, this man looked even smaller sitting there astride this large chestnut horse in his attire of bright red clothes alongside a spacious carriage being harness to two horses.

Behind this carriage were two of the Kings guards who had been sent by the King for the protection of Lady Endevoure and her maid as well as her chattels.

These heavy chattels were tied and situated to the rear of this carriage for the transportation of her Ladyship to the garrison.

Taking his hat from his head then passing it through the air to his waist Vileri with his usual flowery speech announced.

"Welcome glorious Lady your comfortable carriage beckons at your convenience for the alfresco trip to our most wondrous fortress."

Listening to this little man again was beginning to annoy Ordmin as he demanded.

"Stop all your flannel, just dismount and give us a hand with her Ladyships belongings."

Vileri being a diplomat thought it better to obey than to argue against Ordmin, so he dismounted then started to load the carriage with luggage, once loaded he took his hat from his head again followed by his other arm out for the support of Lady Helena allowing her to enter the carriage in comfort.

With Lady Helena and her personal maid now in the carriage she said a last goodbye to her son Gettard before this carriage set off with the escort through the gates of the castle to the forest and beyond.

Chapter Five

Ransomed

The sound of rain outside awakened Gettard very early the next morning in his empty chambers. He was just about to get out of bed when his door flew open; standing there was Ordmin with those two annoying princes' Drago and Hobart hovering directly behind him dressed ready for the morning's training.

"Come on boy on your feet." Ordmin said. "Your training starts today so I suggest you only wear light clothes. Meet us out in the court yard in five minutes?"

With a big stretch followed by a yawn Gettard replied. "Yes sir."

Moving as fast as he could Gettard finally stepped out into the pouring rain where on looking down from the steps he could see Ordmin already had the two youngsters doing extensive exercises on the muddy ground.

With a long stick Ordmin kept prodding the young princes when he thought they were not putting enough effort in to what they were doing. On seeing Gettard at the top of the steps, Ordmin shouted up towards him.

"Come on boy join in and no slacking or I'll make all of you stay out here for the whole day."

It was about an hour that had passed for the three young men, and they were totally soaked and exhausted from Ordmin's continual pressure when suddenly an unruly commotion occurred from where the guards were manning the castle gates.

A bedraggled horse appeared from outside with one of the castle guards slumped over it. The guard was part of the escort that was with Lady Endevoure's group the previous day. He was obviously dead from the amount of arrows protruding from his back.

Seeing this Ordmin with his three students ran over in the mud towards the gates to discover a wet parchment on the guards back under one of the arrows, taking it from this dead man's corps Ordmin decided to read it out loud in front of his students only to find he could just about understand the sodden writing inscribed upon it.

"For the Kings' attention your sister is now our prisoner as punishment for all your atrocities over the past years that you have done to our families. To have her back safely we demand the sum of five hundred gold crowns. Bring this bullion to the first large oak tree that you can see from the cross paths at the west side of Tonest forest before darkness falls tonight. Only one man on horseback or you will never see this Lady again."

Anger with fear raged within the face of young Gettard as he without thinking began to run towards the gates to the outside clearing.

"Stop him!" Ordmin yelled to the two young princes.

Knocking him to the muddy ground from two flying tackles the two Princes dragged Gettard back to face Ordmin.

"Where do you think you are going?" Ordmin said. "You cannot handle this problem alone. You need to calm down before running to become some sort of foolish hero. We must report to the King first of all then we shall work out a plan of action to get your mother back."

The King went into a furious rage as soon as he heard the news of his sisters' kidnap. The thought that someone actually had the audacity to attack his family was too much for him to bear when he said. "Whoever is responsible shall pay with their lives for this action against my family. Ordmin you can have this gold to pay for the ransom, I do not care about the money, either way I shall leave it up to your discretion you can pay these kidnappers or you can kill them, this money is now yours as long as you save Lady Endevoure so that she can carry on with her journey to the garrison."

The King then turned around to one of his trusted servants to go fetch his gold from his private treasury.

To Ordmin this money was no consolation for losing the life of Lady Endevoure he was determined to bring her back safely. He had in his mind devised a plan to free her but needed more men to help him that is why he said to the King. "Sire; May I take your sons along with your nephew Gettard on this mission? The experience will put them all in good stead for their future training."

With a deep stare at Ordmin that would frighten most men the King replied. "You can, but mark my words if anything should befall my sons you shall answer with your own life. To be on the safe side you better take four of my best warriors along with you as an extra precaution. Go now and good hunting."

These warriors of the King were hardened uncouth veterans from many battles they had fought over the past years. They were skilled in archery, jousting and close quarter sword fighting.

Back outside in the castle yard the rain had ceased when Ordmin carrying the bag of gold went to the castle kennels to select himself a tracker dog. Inside the compound of canines he rubbed the bag of gold with some of the straw from the bedding of a bitch on heat. Now with the right dog following the scent on the bag from its mate Ordmin returned to instruct his now dry and fully clothed for battle students on what weapons they should take from the armoury.

Inside the armoury Ordmin pointed towards the weapons that they would need as he explained. "Only take swords, knives and shields, any other weapon would confuse the situation. But before we go charging off I have told the Kings men to give you all a crash course in close quarter fighting."

The four warriors from the King had always used mock fighting as their practise as they did now against these young boys by only using the flat sides of their swords when making their dummy strikes.

With their adrenalin on a high these young students' kept on accidently slipping many times in the mud from the weight of their heavy shields, all three students were beginning to find their own special techniques of fighting in this way.

After a period of time when Ordmin was satisfied with their progress it was time to leave. Walking over to the stables for their horses Ordmin gave a last warning to his students about their adversaries that they were about to meet as he explained. "Whoever it was that wrote that parchment has been well educated so be on your guard, we must be ready to do battle against someone of high birth who is complemented with a lot of intelligence. That is why I have decided to make sure that we have the upper hand by bringing a secret weapon with us." Ordmin then pulled his dog forward with its harness from behind his legs. "Here it is one of the castle's tracker dogs." As the dog came into view it snarled at the young men causing them to jump back in fear of having their legs bitten. "Don't worry he will soon get used to us." Ordmin said as he started to laugh uncontrollably.

King Hagair had always used dogs for hunting in the forest of Tonest, with their strength and good sense of smell they were the ideal solution to Ordmin's immediate problem of affecting this rescue.

Chapter Six

𝔇eath of a 𝔏ady

From their early years of travelling as nomads most of the youngsters in Tonest castle were used to riding horses but not with the extra weight of weapons as these three students found out when they all rode off awkwardly in their saddles from the castle then onwards towards the west side of the forest.

On their arrival a short distance from the cross paths Ordmin gave instructions to his party of rescuers to keep the dog quiet on its leash because he wanted them all to hide in amongst some thick high bushes while he set off on his horse alone to deliver the gold at the delegated oak tree.

Arriving at the cross paths with his horse Ordmin could see the tree in the distance. Its silhouette in front of the falling sun displayed the trees highest branches that were higher than other trees in the area. Riding up to the front of this tree, a familiar voice that Ordmin could not put a face to shouted out of view from above amongst the thick foliage making it impossible for Ordmin to see who this adversary really was.

"Stay on your horse, do not look up into this tree if you value your Lady's life. Now place the bag of gold in that v-shape between those two branches just above your head. Once you have done that wait back at the cross paths until I have instructed my men to release her Ladyship."

Struggling to place a name to the voice Ordmin replied. "If any harm has come to Lady Endevoure I will hunt you down then I shall kill you."

The only response received was silence because no sooner had the gold coinage settled there on its branch when a hand out of sight from Ordmin took it from its perch followed with the sound of a body jumping from the back of the tree as it landed onto a horse.

As horse and rider galloped off into the low sun set it was impossible for Ordmin to see who this man was after he had tried in vain for a look around the large tree trunk, that is when Ordmin had already made up his mind that he was not going to hang around so he rode off back to the bushes where his men were waiting patiently.

Now with the armed force behind him Ordmin on returning back to the tree let their tracker dog pick up the scent from the bag of gold. Now released from its harness the dog was soon off between the trees on to the trail of the kidnappers with the rescuers following closely behind on their horses.

After a short period of time the darkness of night was drawing in when the dog suddenly started barking before disappearing at a clearing over a small hill. With the dog now out of view the rescuers could hear from behind this hill raised voices from the unwelcome presence of this animal.

With the command of dismount from Ordmin the group of men crawled through the wet grass to the ridge of the hill, now looking over from this hill they could just see in the diminishing light the shape of Lady Endevoure's carriage half submerged in a stream with most of its contents scattered in and around the stream, there also to Ordmin's dismay was a group of about twenty men sitting or standing around in front of several fires. At one of these fires their tracker dog was barking at a person who must have had the bag of gold, but there was no sign of it before their dog suddenly yelped; then there was an eerie silence.

From its sudden appearance of this now demised dog which had alerted all those men around their fire's to scan their perimeters hoping to catch sight of anyone who had sent this animal.

Straining his eyes in the diminishing light Ordmin could not see any sight of Lady Endevoure. Turning to his men he asked. "Can any of you see our Lady down there?"

They too after a long peering stare had no luck either at seeing any shapes of a woman amongst the men before replying. "No we cannot, there is no sign of her."

Gettard was now getting anxious of losing his mother, so without thinking he suddenly rose to his feet with his weapon in an effort to charge on down the hill, that's when Ordmin pulled him roughly back to the ground.

"Not yet Gettard wait for my signal."

Then turning to the four men from the King Ordmin commanded.

"Step back from the hill, make a line then give them hell with your arrows."

From the base of the hill these four warriors spread themselves out to form their line as they lifted their bows over their heads from their backs, now with arrows from their quivers set in their bows at forty five degrees fired as many of the arrows as they could into the air to bombard the kidnappers in the clearing the other side of the hill.

From their prone position behind the hill the master and his three students watched the horror unfold as arrows dropped from their highest point before reigning down into human flesh below in the clearing.

Looking back at the Kings men Ordmin gave the order. "Cease fire;" "Grab your horse's men and follow me."

Now on their horses with their weapons at the ready the eight determined fighters rode over the hill with Ordmin leading pointing his sword towards the enemy along with him shouting. "Chaaaaarge;"

A few arrows flew back from their adversaries only to pass over their heads in vein as they rode on valiantly towards their victory.

When the hoofs of their horses trampled the dead or wounded some of the kidnappers decided to run from this onslaught. Those unlucky kidnappers who just stood there rigid with terror in their eyes were quickly killed or wounded from the swords slashing down at them.

There were only four kidnappers who managed to flee into the now darkened forest as Ordmin had just noticed over by the stream the outline of a horse with its rider escaping wearing the same shaped hat that Vileri had worn the day before. It was only then that Ordmin realised whose voice he had listened to in the tree. Vileri!

Before giving chase towards that lone rider Ordmin with his band of victors dismounted as they approached the half submerged carriage only to find inside to their horror the demised bodies of the other guard lying alongside the maid and Lady Endevoure, all three had been brutally beaten before having their throats cut.

Gettard collapsed into the water up to his knees in disbelief at what he was seeing, his only words were. "Mother oh mother;"

At the same time the two princes' vomited uncontrollably at the sight of their aunt's mutilated body.

Ordmin immediately told two of the Kings men to lead his students away from this barbaric catastrophe.

Even though in his heart he had lost someone who had meant the world to him Ordmin still contained a grip on his feelings as he told the remaining men from the King to remove the bodies carefully from the carriage.

After laying the bodies under covers on dry land Ordmin with his men began to harness two of their horses to the carriage to pull it out of the mud.

They were so involved in pushing the carriage from behind that they had missed seeing the carnage that had unfolded not that far from them in the now darkened sky.

Out of sheer revenge for his mother's murder Gettard along with both prince's systematically went about killing of what was left of the wounded enemy that were laying helplessly on the ground in and around the battle area.

The two Kings men who Ordmin had sent away to console them just sat back to let it happen knowing that if they had intervened they were worried that the princes would blacken their name to the King.

When Ordmin eventually found out what they had done he went into an uncontrollable rage as he shouted towards them.

"You idiot's, do you not realise there will be no turning back after this hideous act. These lives you have unnecessarily taken shall scar your minds for life."

This statement from Ordmin was true because from that nights' horror a change for the worst had taken place in each of the young students' characters that would need a very special act of kindness towards each of them to change their attitudes towards their outlook on life.

Before Ordmin turned away from his students in disgust he went on to say. "All of you made this mess now all of you can clean it up, over there are your shields; use them to dig the graves, get on with it."

When all the dead kidnappers were eventually buried Ordmin told everyone that they would wait until daybreak until then they were all told to find a suitable place for sleeping.

With the early morning light showing the blood spattered ground in front of the mounds of earth for the graves this group arose from their sleep to the stern voice of Ordmin. "I have decided that I myself and Gettard will carry on with the hunt for Vileri. The rest of you will take Lady Endevoure along with her maid and guard in the carriage to the barracks, on doing so you shall stay there until we have returned with Vileri. On no account are any of you to go back to the castle until we have completed our mission, do I make myself clear?"

By now they had all realised that Ordmin was not a happy man, that's why tactfully they all understood by just giving a grunt followed with a nod from their heads.

Eventually when they were ready the carriage with its entourage departed towards the garrison while Ordmin with Gettard mounted their horses before speeding off in the other direction in their pursuit of the escaping man called Vileri.

Chapter Seven

The Reckoning

Tracking was not easy for the two hunters but with determination along with luck and sheer instinct the pair discovered at some distance later on the outskirts of the forest the ashes of a fire that Vileri had made to keep himself warm on his escape that last night.

Kneeling down in front of the ashes after dismounting from his horse; Gettard commented. "From the warmth of the embers it seems Vileri is about two hours in front of us, if we keep on going at the speed we are travelling we should, with a bit of luck, catch up with him by the end of the day."

Looking at the tracks in the direction that they should travel Ordmin replied. "I agree but we should still press on carefully because you never know with a slippery fellow like he is he might have left a few surprises in the form of traps to bar our way."

An hour later, riding at a steady pace, Ordmin and Gettard found themselves on the outskirts of a small hamlet consisting of several timber houses, amongst these dwellings was a tavern house for travellers.

Dismounting from their horses just outside the tavern Ordmin with Gettard had to lower their heads as they entered through the small door, once inside they were confronted by several eyes staring back at them in the form of hardened drinkers who were sitting in various places around a medium sized room.

Over at the far end of this room was the owner called Daro Raymond, a short over-sized belly of a man with a bald head sporting a curly beard under a bright red round face wearing an apron. He was standing directly in front of two large barrels of mead. As the two hunters walked through the tables towards this tubby little man Gettard suddenly fell forward to the ground after tripping over a well placed unexpected foot from an ugly looking ruffian sitting at one of the middle tables.

"Hello we have another clumsy Bartie!" This undesirable trouble-maker said.

Gettard drew his sword from its scabbard after picking himself up from the wooden floor with the words. "You silly idiot see if you think this is funny!"

Now with his sword at the man's throat the whole room erupted. All the other drinkers standing up and reaching for their weapons, at the same time a door opened to the rear of the barrels and a tall lanky teenage boy entered into this conflict carrying a tray of warmed up jugs of mead. His name is Cumbart, now, at the age of fourteen after working for a year in this tavern, was the owner's youngest son out of three, with his long yellow hair covering most of his long gaunt face. This boy was known to the locals to be a little clumsy when serving at the tables, his hands with his feet are over-sized making it easy for him to stumble over any furniture he happened to pass.

Noticing trouble was about to explode in his father's tavern Cumbart being more wise than anyone would have realised pretended to trip over someone's foot with the result that all his jugs of mead went flying through the air only to splash down on to the heads of most of his father's customers resulting in cooling them off immediately.

His father stood there in awe at what he had just witnessed as he blurted out. "Oh no, you idiot, not again Bartie will you never learn."

For the name of Bartie being mentioned was all it took for the whole room of customers to lower their weapons as they uncontrollably burst into fits of laughter.

Rising from the floor Cumbart gave a wink to Ordmin as he said. "Don't worry I'm used to being made a fool of its part of my job."

As the room of customers quietened Ordmin with Gettard who had now calmed himself asked the owner Daro Raymond if he had seen a small man in his tavern this day with a peacock feather in his hat called Vileri.

Wiping his hands on his apron Daro replied. "Do you mean that fellow who talks in riddles; yes he was here about an hour ago and looking a bit shifty too."

Ordmin then asked. "Have you any idea in which direction he travelled?"

Before Daro could reply' Cumbart answered for his father. "I know, when serving I overheard him talking to two rough looking locals on how or which was a safe route through the swamp lands. After handing over what looked like a gold coin the two locals left to show the way by travelling with him."

From their first meeting Gettard took to a liking towards Cumbart for his part of avoiding their serious problem on entering in this tavern, this gave him an idea as he said to Ordmin. "Perhaps if Bartie knows he could show us the way through the swamp lands?"

This was a wonderful idea to Cumbart as he would always try to find an excuse for avoiding working in this tavern; he then turned to his father for a positive answer.

"All right but don't take all day I need you back here as soon as possible!" His father said looking as though he had just been conned.

Cumbart led the way on foot with his two companions following on their horses closely behind. Now with the trees behind them the terrain changed as they found the ground they were travelling on was beginning to soften. Turning round to face his riders Cumbart remarked. "I would advise that from this point on dismounting would be a good idea or you will find yourselves sinking into the mud."

As the trio started treading carefully they soon came across the tracks of their adversaries.

After scrutinising these tracks Ordmin came to a conclusion, "It looks from these heavy markings as though Vileri is still riding his horse alongside the tracks of two men walking; it seems his guides have not given him the advice that you gave us."

It was not long after when the three trackers still on boggy ground had rounded a large hill with steep sides that they noticed in the distance Vileri standing on his saddle with his horse underneath him slowly sinking into quicksand.

It seemed that the two undesirable guides had managed to obtain the bag of coins from him while standing back on safer ground as they watched Vileri struggle to save his life from certain death.

Leaving their horses behind Ordmin now with his sword out of its scabbard raced with his two young men towards these rogues, now in front with his sword high Ordmin sliced it down to take the hand off of the man that was holding the coins, with this man screaming with the loss of his hand the other ruffian hit Ordmin on the back of the head with his wooden club before Gettard had a chance to stop him.

With Ordmin out cold in the mud Gettard thrust his sword forward towards this ruffian's body, only to miss by inches as this undesirable turned sideways to avoid his metal blade, now leaning forward Gettard was at a disadvantage as the same club hit him on the back of the head sending him also into the mud. While all this was happening Cumbart on speeding forward happened to trip over Ordmins body sending him head first into the ruffian's chest knocking this adversary backwards into the swamp.

By this time Vileri being frightened was up to his ankles in bog with his poor horse inches away from certain death, the horse had

45

now given up to the elements as it was immersed up to his head in quagmire and was, at this time, frozen with terrible fear. Jumping to his feet from the glancing blow to his head Gettard made sure this time when his sword found its mark in the stomach of his fallen enemy.

With his companion dead the other ruffian holding his blooded stump with his opposite hand ran for his life leaving a trail of blood behind him.

"Help; You have to save me!" These cries came from Vileri as he slowly immersed in the quicksand.

Fearing for Vileri's life Cumbart said. "We must help him!"

With anger still raging in Gettard's eyes he replied. "Forget it, he killed my mother. Let the murderer die, he deserves it, anyway it's too late there is no way of getting him out of there."

With Ordmin lying on the ground still out for the count these two young men helplessly watched Vileri gradually disappear from sight into the quicksand to his ultimate death.

Half an hour had passed when finally Ordmin awoke from his concussion only to find himself lying on his stomach across the back of his own horse with Gettard sitting behind holding the reigns. His first words to Gettard were. "Where's that murderer Vileri?"

Gettard replied immediately. "He's dead!" "He deserved what he got! He disappeared into the quicksand; there was nothing we could do to save him."

It was after that statement from Gettard that Ordmin realised this young boys character had hardened towards life in general.

Lifting his head to the side Ordmin noticed Cumbart riding beside awkwardly on the other horse; it seemed that Cumbart might fly over the horse's head because every now and then he would jerk forward in an unstable movement from the power of this animal.

Sure enough before long it happened Cumbart accident prone as he was, suddenly went flying in a summersault over the horses head only to land on his bottom, that's when Ordmin demanded to be let down off his horse to see if Cumbart was injured.

"Can you stand Cumbart or do you need help?" Ordmin said while looking concerned that this young man might have broken one of his bones.

Before Cumbart could answer; Gettard interrupted when he said. "Of course he's all right he has got to get used to riding if he is to become my friend."

Looking at these two young men gave Ordmin an idea that Cumbart would make a good companion for Gettard in his training to become a knight.

Helping Cumbart to his feet Ordmin said to him. "Would you like to live at the castle with Gettard to train in the art of battle skills? It will not be easy but you shall be fed regularly with good sleeping quarters. If you agree I shall talk to your father to see if he will release you from your work to let you go."

Cumbart could not have foreseen this future in his life, but the thought of escaping from his mundane lifestyle in his father's tavern appealed to him so much that his answer was an immediate. "Yes I would."

As soon as Ordmin had his answer he changed the subject because he had just remembered about the bag of gold coins. "I don't suppose you both remembered to pick up those gold coins when leaving that swamp, did you?"

Gettard turned around in his saddle and pointed to the bag tied to one of the horses straps. "Yes we did sir we are not that daft even if you think we are."

Giving an embarrassing small cough along with a nod Ordmin reclaimed his horse while the young men both rode together on the other horse so that they could make their way back to the tavern.

Half an hour later on entering this tavern belonging to the Raymond family Ordmin after a time managed to persuade Cumbart's father that it would be in his own interests for the future of his family to let Cumbart go to live at Tonest castle.

After a good solid meal supplied by their host it was agreed that Ordmin with Gettard would ride on to the garrison; leaving Cumbart to stay with his family for a week before making his trip to change his life for his future as a warrior at Tonest castle.

Chapter Eight

𝕱𝖎𝖌𝖍𝖙 𝖆𝖙 𝖙𝖍𝖊 𝕲𝖆𝖗𝖗𝖎𝖘𝖔𝖓

On the hill looking out above the beautiful clearing where the garrison was situated, Ordmin and Gettard sat there for a moment on their weary horses to admire the construction of this fortress.

After pondering for some time Ordmin eventually said. "I hope the King's sons are behaving themselves in there otherwise that Lord Darnley can be a little bit strict when it comes to keeping order in his garrison."

"Well he will have his hands full knowing what those two prince's are like." Gettard replied as he dug his stirrups into the sides of his horse and moving forward down the hill with Ordmin towards the large gates of the garrison.

Now inside the gates these two weary travellers rode through the settlement of houses towards the manor house where Lord Darnley was standing on his steps after being alerted by his lookouts.

"Welcome we've been waiting for you to arrive. Did you succeed in your pursuit of the murderous Vileri?"

Ordmin replied as he and Gettard dismounted from their horses. "Yes we did; He is not coming back, he is dead."

Lord Darnley then said. "Well that is a shame I would have liked to have known the reason he did it, now we will never know."

He then ordered two of his servants to take the horse's reins from his visitors, at the same time he placed his hand on Gettard's shoulder before saying. "We had no idea that Vileri was plotting to kidnap your mother. He has been in our service for two years, in that time we have had no problems from him. My daughter and I myself are very sorry for the death of your mother, if you follow me I shall take you to her where she is lying in the manor's chapel of rest."

While Lord Darnley was occupied he had made sure his servants had led Ordmin along the corridor with his bag of gold coins towards the sleeping quarters where he was united with his student prince's who were at this time arguing about whose turn it was to have the cot laden with straw out of four positioned by the window.

Apparently Prince Drago had slept in this cot the night before, now his brother thought it was his turn.

This was not what Ordmin needed as he was very tired from the last two days that is why he raised his voice in anger against his King's two sons. "What are you both griping about now, it's time that you both started to grow up or you will never become Knights."

After bringing order within their quarters Ordmin hid his gold coins within the straw on his allotted cot, at the same time back at the chapel Lord Darnley left Gettard to be alone with his mother so that he could say his last goodbyes.

That evening everyone attended a meal in the great hall at the manor.

Long tables were situated around the perimeters of this great hall.

Lord Darnley sat at the head table with his daughter Silvianda on his right, Ordmin and Gettard to his left.

This was the first time Gettard had seen Silvianda, the sight of her sent a warm glow inside his body, and he had never seen such a lovely young girl in all his life.

To the disappointment of Lord Darnley the amorous Prince Drago managed to claim the seat next to Silvianda whereas Prince Hobart sat as far away as he could from his brother by sitting next to Gettard.

Before their food was served by the castle servants Lord Darnley stood to his feet to say a few words on behalf of Gettard's mother.

"For all of you who knew Lady Endevoure let us remember her by lifting our goblets in a toast for her sad parting from this world; 'Rest in peace Lady Helena Endevoure.'"

Tears appeared in Gettard's eyes as Ordmin out of view gave Gettard's arm a light squeeze of reassurance before sitting down with the rest of the diners.

It was not long after all the food had been brought in when, after tucking in to this feast, Gettard noticed out the corner of his eye Prince Drago, who whilst eating, was pestering Silvianda in an uncomfortable way, nudging even closer from his seat to hers so that she was almost slipping the other way off from her own seat.

Seeing this Gettard became annoyed at this Prince as he finally snapped by shouting. "Leave the girl alone, let her eat, she does not want you pestering her all the time."

Standing to his feet Prince Drago scowled back at Gettard before saying.

"Why don't you mind your own business orphan boy?"

Being in the middle of this mêlée Lord Darnley being unhappy stood up on to his feet. "Silence, we do not argue at meal times, if you want to fight you shall do it in a civilised way. I suggest that tomorrow morning in the manor's yard you shall both settle your differences with an organized fight. That is if Ordmin decides to agree to it."

To Ordmin this was a good idea, it was just what these two young men needed to take their minds off of the last several days.

"Good idea Lord Darnley; But they should settle their differences after the funeral of Lady Endevoure." Ordmin said then went on to say. "No weapons only with fists will be allowed, we do not need anyone being killed in this duel do we."

There was no arguing now for these two young men after their row had been decided for them they would now have to go through with it if they were to save face in the eyes of the young Silvianda.

Prince Drago while eating was now sitting at a proper distance from the young girl as he had now decided that he would never forgive Gettard for his outburst in showing him up in front of her.

To lord Darnley in his mind he could not thank Gettard enough for his intervention against Prince Drago in keeping him away from his daughter that is why from this day on he took a liking towards this young boy.

One thing was for sure Silvianda had just realised that Gettard had some sort of feelings for her when he tried to protect her from this unruly Prince.

Back inside their sleeping quarters after that evening's meal you could cut the air with a knife as the four visitors to the garrison retired to their cots without saying a single word to each other.

That very next morning as the light appeared from the darkness of the night, Gettard was already exercising by running around the outside perimeter of the garrison in readiness for his forthcoming fight when suddenly Silvianda wearing a hooded cloak that was hiding her head from recognition approached him from the gates of the garrison.

"You must not fight the Prince! He is ready to kill you. He has a knife hidden within his boot." Silvianda said while standing in front of Gettard's run.

"How do you know this?" Gettard gasping for air was surprised at the appearance of this beautiful girl as she went on to say.

"A servant boy had seen him just a moment ago when passing the armoury."

"Thank you Silvianda I'll have to be on my guard, now you had better return before someone recognizes you out here."

As Gettard's eyes watched Silvianda beautifully shaped body walk back through the gates of the garrison he thought to himself. "She must really like me to warn me like that."

After his run Gettard joined the procession of his mother's funeral which took place outside at a hill to the rear of the garrison. With a successful burial Ordmin again said a few words over this grave.

An hour later within the garrison Lord Darnley told his servants to organise the area in which the two young men were to fight.

Around this area standing was the majority population of the garrison in ready for the forthcoming fight, they did not have long to wait when out from the manor doors appeared Gettard with Prince Drago stripped to their waists wearing only but their breaches along with their hands wrapped in rags to protect their knuckles from any injury that they were about to sustain.

Directly behind them was Lord Darnley followed by his entourage of the inhabitants of this manor including his visitors; Ordmin, the other Prince' Hobart and the remainder of the Kings warriors.

Now inside the area these two contenders squared up to one another as they traded punch for punch in a vicious battle with eventually Prince Drago squeezing Gettard in a bear hug around his waist after charging unexpectedly towards him.

Gasping for air after being lifted from the ground Gettard gave a rabbit punch on both ears in response to his opponents move only to send this Prince back holding his ears in agony to the ground.

"Ouch that hurt you bloody rat!" Prince Drago said as his hand dropped secretly down to find the knife from within his boot, with a sudden forward thrust of his arm this knife just missed Gettard's groin as this young man stepped sideways out of reach of his opponent's dangerous knife plunge.

It was a good job that Silvianda had warned Gettard to be on his guard because without hesitation Gettard lifted his foot from the ground to the side of the Prince's hand only to kick this knife out of his hand by shoving the point upwards into the air.

As Prince Drago had lurched forward on to his stomach with his thrust, the knife somersaulted in flight to return point downwards towards his exposed back.

The onlooker's around the area gasped in horror at what was about to happen until Gettard's quick response of swiping his hand across the path of the blade caused it to change direction out of harm's way.

With a slight cut to his hand Gettard stepped back to allow Prince Drago to rise to his feet then with a flurry of punches to the Prince's body he sent him back to the ground again, now on his knees winded Prince Drago out of sight scooped up a handful of dust then threw it into Gettard's eyes blinding him temporally.

With his eyes stinging Gettard received two punches to his chin from Prince Drago after this young prince had managed to rise from his winded state. This gave him time to rush back over to pick up the knife again only to find that Gettard who was partly blinded had managed to fly through the air towards him in the hope of stopping the knife from being used again.

Now with both young men in a wrestling match on the ground Gettard managed to grab Prince Drago around his neck with his arms in a strangle hold along with his legs trapping Prince Drago's arm against his body in a scissors lock making it impossible for him to move out of this position.

Blood was now oozing from the corner of Gettard's mouth as he tightened his hold making it impossible for this Prince to breathe, now gasping for air Prince Drago started to lose consciousness that is when Lord Darnley had seen enough, for fear of damage to this Prince he decided to send Ordmin into the area to stop this fight.

Standing to their feet out of their clench after Ordmin had separated these young men Ordmin told them to shake each other's hands. With his hand out Gettard received a slap to his hand from Prince Drago along with the words. "Forget it, this is not over, I'll teach you never to strike a prince. When my father hears of this you will wish you had never been born."

From this threat Prince Drago turned then walked off dejected pushing through the onlookers towards the manor house.

Ordmin was upset at Prince Drago for not being man enough in defeat so he said to Gettard. "Don't worry son I shall inform his majesty of what really happened here today, he is not going to be happy about your mother's death along with his son's dishonourable behaviour."

With Prince Drago out of the way the spectators rushed forward to congratulate the triumphant Gettard with several slaps to his back for his win.

While all this was happening Prince Drago back at their quarters took the opportunity of gathering his personal belongings, as he was doing this he remembered the bag of gold coins that Ordmin had hidden the day before. Sorting through the straw on his master's cot he finally found this bag' once in his possession he rapidly made his way out from the manor in secret to the stables where he saddled his horse before mounting it along with his luggage and swag.

Now outside on his horse Prince Drago dug his heels into this horse to race through the dwellings towards the gates of the garrison before anyone had a chance of stopping him.

Hobart not interested in congratulating Gettard happened to see his brother's escape while standing outside the area before deciding to shout a warning to alert everyone. "My brother is riding off!"

As they all turned in response to his voice Lord Darnley said. "Let him go it's no good trying to stop him he is used to running away from us to disappear outside there somewhere."

"I agree he will return one day when he is ready to." Ordmin replied as he started to walk back to the manor to see at what Prince Drago had been up to.

Inside their sleeping quarters Ordmin with his students were confronted with straw sprawled across the floor where this Prince had rummaged into Ordmin's cot before finding the bag of gold.

Being despondent with all that had happened in the last few days Ordmin moaned. "Oh no that young thief has stolen my money, he better stay away otherwise I will not be responsible for my actions."

Prince Hobart made matters worse when he remarked. "You would not have had that money anyway if you had paid the ransom like you were told to do. So you cannot blame my brother for taking this money when it belongs to my family anyway."

Even though this young Prince was right Ordmin found it was hard burden to bear especially as the King had told him that he could keep this money if he was to bring Vileri to justice. That is why he decided to change the subject when he said. "It is time we travelled back to the castle this afternoon so gather your things then meet me with the King's men by the stables after I have informed Lord Darnley of our departure.

Now on their horses beside the recovered carriage Ordmin with his group said their goodbyes to Lord Darnley who was standing there on the steps of the manor with his daughter. As Gettard rode off, this young man was sure he had seen a tear trickling down the cheeks of Silvianda. Looking down from the hill overlooking the garrison Gettard looked back then said to Ordmin. "One day I shall take that young girl for my wife." Ordmin being surprised at this statement said. "Do not let the King hear you say that he would like that girl to marry his son, so don't get your hopes up."

"We'll see, time will tell," Gettard replied as he rode onward behind the carriage.

Chapter Nine

Revenge of a King

The fortress was a welcome site to Ordmin and his group of weary travellers. They entered the safety of the castle grounds before dismounting from their horses and leading them to the stables.

Now walking across the yard and entering the door to the corridor, Ordmin with his students reported directly to their King who was at the time sitting behind his large table within the great hall.

"Have you news of my sister?" The King asked.

Ordmin who reluctantly replied was standing in front of this table with his students who were looking on directly behind him. "I have Sire; there is no easy way of telling you."

"What is it, just tell me?" The King snapped with impatience for an answer.

"Lady Endevoure is dead, murdered by her escort Vileri and his band of cut throats. We arrived too late, the only consolation is we tracked them all down then killed them."

"So where is my sister? Did you bring her body back here?"

"No Sire Lady Endevoure is buried in the garrison's grave yard."

King Hagair sat there staring into thin air for almost a minute until suddenly he shook himself out of this trance when he said to Ordmin. "Apparently not all of these kidnappers are dead, it seems that poor wretch I have in my dungeons did tell my jailors the truth then."

Beginning to get a little worried Ordmin asked.

"Your majesty who is it you have?"

With his eyes watering this King answered. "Yesterday a rough looking man with a blood soaked stump instead of his hand came to the castle looking for Cretorex the medicine man. When Cretorex was cauterizing his arm he actually boasted that he knew who had killed an important lady. After finding this out from Cretorex I had this idiot of a rogue arrested, then with some persuasion we managed to get the truth out of him."

As soon as the King had finished his story he turned to his guards.

"Go and get the prisoner, bring him here now?"

There was silence in the great hall as Ordmin with his students waited anxiously for the return of these guards.

The King just sat there now with anger in his eyes from knowing the true fate of his younger sister.

Suddenly the silence was broken from the screams from behind the doors outside in the corridor as this ruffian was dragged towards the great hall.

Now inside it was obvious that this poor devil had been tortured, his face was covered in blood along with severe bruises to his neck where he had been stretched on the rack, his fingers to his only hand was minus its nails from all being pulled out with farriers' pliers.

Now being forced to his knees by the guards in front of the King, this King asked Ordmin. "Is this one of the kidnappers?"

"No sire he is a robber who stole the ransom money from Vileri."

That's all it took to condemn this ruffian when the king just nodded to his guards before they dragged this poor soul still on his knees to the centre of the hall still screaming for mercy.

Then a heavy double edged sword was taken from one of the corners of the hall by one of these guards who brought it back before bringing it down with a quick swipe squarely across the back of this unlucky fellow's neck which immediately took his head off?

Once off this head rolled spilling blood into the cracks of the halls stoned floor. At the same time blood shot upwards like a fountain from the veins of the remaining torsos neck.

From complete shock of what had just occurred Gettard along with Hobart averted their eyes from this horror, that is when the King said to them. "How dare you look away, look, this is what happens for allowing someone to escape after you completed your mission. You boys are lucky that I did not have your master beheaded for his negligence. Now all of you get out and don't come back until I call for you."

Ordmin gave a gulp at his King's suggestion of taking his life as he himself and his students bowed while backing off towards the double doors to make their escape from their Kings wrath.

Before they departed the King asked one more question. "By the way where is my son Drago?"

This was the one question Ordmin was dreading when he tactfully answered. "Sire your son the Prince took it on himself to depart from the garrison early. We have no idea as to where he has gone."

The King made an ahm sound as he gestured with the back of his hand for the three to depart.

On leaving outside in the corridor Hobart complained to Ordmin. "Never once did my father ask how I got on, it's almost as though he had disowned me."

Knowing that this boy would always report back to his father, Ordmin was careful with the reply he gave him when he replied. "One day you will have your chance to show him what you can do, once you have been taught all the skills of becoming a Knight, and then he will appreciate you more as an honourable son."

Two days later when all the fuss had quietened the two students were now in their newly obtained dormitory supplied by the Kings servants who had worked tirelessly in last few days to combine Gettard's old chambers with other rooms that were lying vacant.

The next morning after Ordmin had aroused the two students from their cots they were both now outside the castle grounds learning their battle skills under his tuition when they suddenly noticed Cumbart running down towards them from the forest at the top of the hill.

The outline of his body was easily recognised, being so lanky; each step of his run was awkward but so fast that he almost looked as though he would topple over his own feet at any moment.

His actions became clear when behind him out of the forest a bare back rider on a grey stallion was galloping after him at such speed it was obvious that now free of the forest Cumbart was about to be caught.

It was when this rider stood up on to the back of his horse that Gettard realised that from the clothes this man was wearing he was a gypsy or as some people would say a man of the road.

His short black curly hair over a sharp parrot shaped nose with a square jaw line complemented his five foot six inch, broad body, also his colourful patterned cravat along with his bright red shirt over his tanned britches that were kept up by a large buckled belt. He was about to jump, wearing his brown flowery boots, from his steed onto the escaping Cumbart.

Until this same horse suddenly stumbled over some lose pebbles sending this gypsy flying from his standing position into the back of Cumbart's body.

Now sitting in front of each other, one holding his head with the other holding his back these two young lads decided to wrestle each other in the long grass until Ordmin arrived after running up the hill with his students in the hope of stopping this fight.

Ordmin said after finally managing to pull these two apart by grabbing their neck bands. "What is all this about then?"

This gypsy now choking from Ordmin's firm grip replied. "This crook has just stolen my sister's gold bangle I am trying to get it back."

"No I did not she has made it up all because I refused her advances towards me." Cumbart said trying to catch his breath from his exhausting run.

This created a quick response from the gypsy with lunge towards Cumbart along with the words. "You bloody liar!"

Ordmin held his grip as he said. "That's enough you two, there's only one way to solve this is to go back into the forest to find your sister and see if we can resolve this problem in a peaceful way without anyone harming themselves."

With the grey horse now standing from its fall, Gettard grabbed its reins before it had a chance to canter off.

Taking these reins from Gettard this gypsy agreed to Ordmin's suggestion.

Now following this gypsy, Ordmin after ten minutes of walking between the trees with his group of young men finally arrived at a clearing in this forest.

Down in this clearing they could see several carriages that were encircled around a large camp fire with family groups of gypsies going about their daily chores.

By the time Ordmin with his students had arrived down at edge of these carriages a group of gypsies had formed with the head man standing in front this group in ready to see why his camp had been approached by intruders.

"What do you want and why has my son brought you here?" The head man demanded.

Now being encircled by these gypsies Ordmin replied to this head man. "My name is Ordmin from Tonest castle we are here to find out the truth in a dispute between this boy and one of my students. It seems that this lad from your camp has accused our new lad Cumbart of stealing a gold bangle from his sister."

The head man turned to one of his men before saying. "Tell Juniper to come here, we shall see who is telling the truth."

While his man was away collecting the girl the head man told Ordmin his name was Bran Blades, then explained to him that the gypsy boy in front of them was his only son called Fendale who was under Bran's orders to protect his sister at all times.

Ordmin in answer to Bran stated that these students were under his charge and he was personally responsible for their actions.

Two minutes later a young small gypsy girl appeared in front of her father; her pixie looking face was the colour of red cherries from embarrassment to be standing in front of so many men. Her hair was the colour of copper with its long wavy gloss reaching down to her petite waist. She was, by this time, petrified at what her father was about to ask. "Now Juniper tell us the truth did this boy take your bangle or are you making it up?"

Juniper, knowing that her father would eventually subtract the truth from her, looked to the floor in disgrace as she replied. "No he did not take it I made it up because Fendale kept on at me for being with a non gypsy, I'm sorry father."

It was obvious to Ordmin that this girl was a lot younger than Hobart as her father sent her back in disgrace to her carriage. That was also when Bran said to Ordmin. "Because of my sons mistake please accept my apology for any harm he may have caused towards your young man."

Stroking his beard in thought then looking to Cumbart, Ordmin replied. "My student Cumbart accepts your apology, that is right isn't it Cumbart?"

"Yes sir!" Cumbart said after realising he just had a lucky escape from being accused of thieving.

An idea had just come to Ordmin as he said to his students. "Right you lot go back to the castle and carry on with your training while I talk to this man."

With his students gone Ordmin walked down with Bran to sit in front of the camp fire where he made an agreement with this gypsy that he would make sure that his family of Romany's would be allowed to roam in the lands of Tonest in exchange for taking his son Fendale for special training because he could see a lot of potential in this young lad's abilities as he had noticed his skills in horse riding.

After his father had agreed to let his son go, Fendale who was excited at his future prospects of becoming a Knight followed Ordmin towards the castle for his very first day of training.

Mixed feelings towards this new boy called Fendale were in the minds of all the student's as Ordmin returned with him to the exterior of the castle that day.

After a hard day of training, Ordmin was now satisfied with their progress of mixing in as a group of young warriors for his Kings future prospect to form an elite group of knights for protecting the castle of Tonest.

That night in the student's dormitory Cumbart along with Fendale chose their individual cots that were situated next to one another after eventually making friends from their very first day of training.

Chapter Ten

𝔅isthion's 𝔇omain

Two years had passed in the castle; in that time other young men had come and gone after not being suitable for this special type of training.

But in this time the four original students had now mastered many aspects in the art of warfare, they did not know it now but in the years ahead they would all be sent on different quests for their King with the prospect of becoming Knights.

Then one day Gettard, reluctantly, was selected, together with his troublesome cousin Prince Hobart, for one of these quests.

They were told by their King to go and help a small community of people who were being harassed from a creature called a Bisthion which the rumour had it was running around wild causing damage to crops and live stock in an area of Vorth some three hours distance, to the east of the castle.

To help them in their quest they were instructed to take Cretorex, the medicine man along with them as he had now established himself at being good at diagnosing most ailments along with having some knowledge of how certain animal's minds worked.

After gathering their weapons from the castle armoury consisting of swords, shields and spears, these three travellers with their horses set off through the castle gates on their journey in the early hours just as the morning light appeared over the horizon.

After travelling some distance through two forests along with one grass plain they finally arrived at a farm house on the outskirts of the district called Vorth.

Dismounting from his horse while the two students sat on theirs;

Cretorex knocked on the farmhouse door only to find that there was no response, then turning to face the young students he said. "I expect the land owner is out there somewhere farming, we should ride on until we see someone."

It was not long before the three riders noticed a cloud of dust in a distant field, out of this cloud after closer inspection by riding nearer they discovered a herd of stampeding cattle had already started escaping from a massive beast, this animal with the head of a bull along with the body of a lion was actually in the process of flattening before mounting one of these poor cows.

Behind the cloud of dust they also noticed the land owner was trying desperately to beat this animal with a stick in the hope of separating this beast from his exhausted cow.

Cretorex, looking worried said. "That man is a fool he should keep clear of that animal it is very dangerous to intervene when a bull of some type is mating."

As soon as Cretorex had finished these words, Gettard heeled his horse as he sped off in the direction of this Bisthion in the hope of attracting the attention of this beast away from doing anymore damage.

"Let the idiot kill; himself." The Prince said to Cretorex while thinking to himself. "Rather him than me."

Cretorex concerned for Gettard's safety replied. "That foolhardy boy will get us all killed, come on let us go and help him before he adds to the damage that is already being done."

By the time Gettard had ridden up to the Bisthion it had already finished its indulgence with the cow and was now aiming its horns towards the defending land owner.

Now riding up beside this Bisthion, Gettard using his spear tapped this beast on its rump in the hope of distracting it away from its quarry.

It worked because as soon as it felt the spear against its body the Bisthion turned its head around with a toss only to gash the side of Gettard's horse with its horns.

By the time Cretorex and the Prince had arrived, the horse of Gettard's had already reared up in pain before speeding off with its rider while being chased by the Bisthion.

Checking first that the land owner was not injured, Cretorex asked the man what the terrain was like in the direction that the young rider was heading for.

Cretorex was informed by this man that they should both ride as fast as they could to save their friend from falling to his death at the edge of the canyon of Vorth where this land owner also believed this Bisthion originally came from.

With the ground rising on a gradual slope then suddenly, to find a shear drop in front of him, Gettard managed to steer his horse by the reins just in time before his ultimate demise of falling off the cliffs edge to this canyon.

The Bisthion was not so lucky, still charging forward with its heavy weight was unable to turn in time as it leaped into the air before falling to its untimely death. By this time Cretorex arrived alone on the scene without Prince Hobart who had taken it on himself to go and find a way down into this canyon for trophy hunting.

"Gettard are you injured in anyway?" Cretorex asked who at this time was more worried for Gettard's injured horse as he dismounted to have a look at this poor animals gash.

"No I am fine." Gettard replied as he jumped from one horse to the other.

"Hope you don't mind me using your horse? I would like to see what that Prince is up to." Gettard said as he sped off in the direction of Prince Hobart.

Just around the perimeter of this canyon Gettard came across a hidden steep narrow track leading down to the base of this canyon's expanse.

While riding down this track at a careful pace he noticed a female Bisthion with her young calf just outside several caves in the distance to the rear of this canyon.

By the time Gettard had finally reached the base of the canyon he found the dead male Bisthion laying there from its fatal fall before noticing in the distance the Prince was holding his spear in the throwing position while charging on his horse towards a mother Bisthion and its calf in the hope of killing them.

Even when Gettard started to ride towards the Prince in the hope of saving this family of Bisthions, Prince Hobart had already thrown his spear which was now embedded, just above the eyes, in the forehead of the mother killing her instantly only to leave her calf standing there at the mercy of this Prince's blood let.

Now dismounting from his horse with his sword in his hands above his head this Prince prepared to take the head off of this young calf until, in the nick of time, Gettard had jumped from his horse and managed to save the offending blow by parrying Prince Hobart's sword, from underneath, with his own sword with the affect of sending the sharpened blade into the air.

"What do you think you are doing you idiot?" The Prince said as he was very upset at losing an extra trophy for his father's castle.

"We can't kill this calf it could be the last of its kind." Gettard replied, who was now standing between the calf and the Prince.

Now losing his temper Prince Hobart charged head first into Gettard's stomach sending both boys into a wrestling match on the ground. It seemed like five minutes in a stale mate of struggling between these two when Cretorex arrived on the scene with the other horse. Dismounting he reached for his brown cloth bag attached to his waist which he used for its contents of powder to throw over these two fighters, sending them both into a comatose sleep.

Now with these two scrappers out for the count Cretorex examined the calf for any injuries that it might have sustained from its mother falling down dead beside it.

After an hour Gettard with Prince Hobart awoke to the contented noises that the calf was making as it suckled the udders of a cow that the land owner had brought down into the canyon on Cretorex's request.

That is when Cretorex said to these two angry young men. "Right you two this land owner has agreed to look after this calf until it lives to maturity. We have both agreed that it should be secured with a fence on the track to let it stay down here in this canyon to live out its days in safety until it dies."

Gettard now beginning to come round as he staggered to his feet replied. "Who is going to feed it once it is down here?"

Cretorex then went on to say that the land owner would be rewarded in kind if he agreed to keep this animal fed in fodder for the rest of its days as long as someone from the castle would visit from time to time to see if this Bisthion was well secured.

This was something that Gettard was willing to do as long as Ordmin agreed to it seeing that it was not in their syllabus of training.

Picking up his sword, Prince Hobart decided he could not wait to reclaim his trophies as he was about to take the head off of the female Bisthion's carcass until Cretorex stopped him when he said. "Hobart why take the heads off now when we could travel on to the garrison where they have the facilities of their butchers who could process this meat tidily, then you can have your heads taken off professionally with no mess involved."

Reluctantly the Prince agreed as they all started to make two stretchers out of wood for carrying the dead Bisthion's.

The stretchers now being towed behind two of their horses these three adventurers made their way back to the garrison with the prospect of a slap up meal from the meat that they were carrying.

On their way to the garrison Prince Hobart was muttering to himself in a peculiar way which unsettled Gettard in as much that he thought the Prince was plotting revenge towards him for depriving him of a third trophy. Little did he know that in the years to come this Prince would be more devious than he could have ever imagined.

Chapter Eleven

Return as a Knight

After an hour's ride the view of the garrison's timber walls was a welcoming sight for Gettard as he was now looking forward to seeing Silvianda again.

Once inside this fortress Cretorex and his young men were greeted with cheers from the residents who were all happy to see this fresh meat enter into their community as did Lord Darnley when he greeted these three from the stone steps at his manor.

"Welcome my friends; I see you have brought your dinner with you."

Lord Darnley said as his mouth started to dribble at the thought of eating all that succulent meat that he was now looking at.

"Yes sir." Cretorex replied then went on to say as he and his companions dismounted from their horses. "Perhaps you could tell us were your butchers are so that Hobart can instruct them on how to cut off his trophies for taking back to the castle?"

Now with his stomach rumbling from hunger Lord Darnley replied.

"My own cooks can sort out your meat, just leave it to them they know what to do. If the Prince wants to go to the kitchens he just has to follow them. In the mean time my servants will show you all to your quarters for the night. Later we shall indulge ourselves with a feast from that game that you have brought us."

That evening in the great hall it was wonderful for Gettard as he was allowed to sit next to Silvianda, it was more than two years from when he had last laid eyes on her. The young lady seemed to be lovelier than ever from when they last met.

Her smile with her beautiful looks sent a warm glow inside Gettard. He now realised he had fallen in love for the very first time.

Lord Darnley noticed this attraction of fondness between his daughter and this young man, to him he preferred Gettard as her suitor rather than the instability of Prince Dago's disappearing acts.

So looking towards them he said. "Gettard perhaps you would like to escort Silvianda for a ride tomorrow? It would be good for her to get out of this garrison for a change of scenery."

These two youngsters' faces lit up at the thought of being allowed to have their freedom together as Gettard replied. "Yes Sir as long as Cretorex agrees to it as I am under his charge."

This statement gave Cretorex a sense of self respect from this young man when he gave his permission to Gettard as long as he promised not to stay out for more than two hours.

Prince Hobart who was sitting the other side Cretorex had frowned in disapproval at what he had just heard, in his mind it would be more ammunition he could use against them for keeping in his father the Kings' good books.

The sun was out early the next morning as Gettard rode off with Silvianda out through the gates of the garrison to the green fields situated in front of the backdrop of trees in the distance.

After riding for some distance these two friends took time out to sit in the long grass after dismounting from their horses.

As they sat their getting to know each other by talking about their likes and dislikes they failed to see a lone figure in the distance sitting there upon his charger watching every move that they made.

It was when Gettard decided it was time to make their way back to the garrison that this rider decided to charge towards Gettard's horse as he was trying to help Silvianda to mount up on hers.

As Gettard was sent flying to the ground he noticed the rider was in full armour which was the colour of silver while holding a shield with a red dragon displayed within it, his helmet with its visor down sported a red plum above it.

Taking the reins of Silvianda's horse the Knight cantered off pulling her mount with her still in the saddle as she shouted for help.

Standing to his feet before mounting his own horse Gettard rode off in pursuit of this Knight.

It did not take him long to catch up to this kidnapper as the weight of this Knight's armour was slowing him down.

Jumping on top of the Knight from his own horse, Gettard unbalanced this rider by sending them both tumbling to the ground with a massive thud, at the same time the Knight's shield flew off in the other direction into the grass.

By this time Silvianda's horse veered to one side from the sudden pull of its rein then from there slid to the ground on its side taking her with it together with her yelling out an almighty scream.

As she lay there with her leg trapped under the horse Gettard was desperately trying to lift the visor to this Knight's helmet.

"Gettard help me I can't move?" She cried as she was now worried in case her horse was to roll over on top of her.

"Hold on I'm coming." Replied Gettard, who was now surprised when the Knight managed to roll on top of him.

Now pinned to the ground from the weight, the Knight decided to punch Gettard on the chin with his clenched fisted gauntlet along with the words of. "No you don't not if I get to her first."

As this Knight moved towards Silvianda, Gettard who was stunned momentarily from the punch still found it in himself to overcome the blow as he reached out to grab the Knight's shield, without thinking Gettard with one hand let go of this shield in a discus throw as it finally sliced the back of this Knight's ankle sending him sprawling head first to the ground again.

Gettard then ran over stepping on the back of the Knight's helmet, pushing his head into the earth, thus clogging up the slits in his visor as he tried in vain to see what Gettard's next move was.

If he had he would have seen Gettard raise Silvianda's horse with her still on it, then with a slap to its rump Gettard sent the horse on its way in the direction of the garrison.

Meanwhile the knight lifted his visor then rushed over to his horse for his double edged sword. After taking his sword out of its scabbard the Knight then turned holding it high towards Gettard in the hope of striking him down with a fatal blow.

This never came as Gettard was quick on his feet as he lifted the shield from the ground again and parried the blow, and then taking the shield in two hands swiped it sideways across the Knight's helmet taking it off only to reveal his nemesis Prince Drago. Now knocked back sideways on to the floor the Prince was helpless as Gettard sat across him with the edge of his own shield against the prince's throat.

Now with the upper hand Gettard took the opportunity to demand.

"Do you yield Sir Knight or do I take your life, the decision is yours?"

Prince Drago thinking to him himself he would rather be around to fight another day decided it in his own interest to surrender when he replied to Gettard. "I yield this time but I will be back."

With that statement Gettard hit Prince Drago across the head with the flat of the shield knocking him out cold with the words of. "That is up to you, you idiot."

Leaving the Prince there to recover, Gettard now back on his horse sped off in the direction of the garrison to his beloved Silvianda.

Just outside the garrison, Gettard managed to catch up with Silvianda. Now riding alongside her he explained why this Knight had attacked them.

For her own safety he made up a story that he had known this Knight before when in his training as a student at the castle had discovered him to be a bad loser after they had fought each other. Gettard also explained that this Knight had sworn he would one day find a way of getting his revenge on him.

After reassuring Silviander that she would be quite safe now, these two eventually found their way back into the safety of the garrison.

Once Gettard had left Silviander at her quarters he made an appointment to see Lord Darnley and explain to him at what Prince Drago had been up to, after a lengthy discussion they decided to keep it a secret from Silvianda of who the Knight really was.

But Lord Darnley did promise he would now always make sure that Silvianda would have an escort when she left the garrison.

The next day was time to leave for Cretorex and his young men as they collected their stretchers full of processed meat before attaching them to their horses.

Before leaving Gettard promised Silvianda he would try to visit her whenever he had a chance to.

All this attention towards this beautiful girl had not gone unnoticed by Prince Hobart who was now plotting some sort of scheme to take Gettard under his control.

After saying goodbye to Lord Darnley standing there on his steps with his daughter beside him the trio made their way back to their castle.

Sometime later as they were travelling Prince Hobart on his horse sided up to Gettard for a quiet word so as not to let Cretorex hear, he said. "If you do not want me to tell the King about your affair with Silvianda I would advise you that you owe me one in the future when I shall need your services."

Gettard ignored this comment made by the Prince; he thought he would not give the Prince the satisfaction of letting him know that he really cared.

If he had replied to the Prince's comment it would have only added fuel to the fire.

Chapter Twelve

The Inauguration

Back at their castle there was something odd within the walls as the three travellers passed through the drawbridge gates, there were no guards to be seen up on the ramparts, the only people to be seen were two stable hands who were looking as though they were near deaths door, sweating profusely they just about managed to drag themselves forward to take hold of the reigns of these three incoming horses.

Cretorex, looking down at one of these poor wretches said. "You don't look very well, where is everyone?"

The poor man could just about speak as he said. "There is a fever in the castle, most of us have got it and there are only a few that have escaped this sickness who are trying to help the rest of us."

Dismounting from their horses Cretorex then asked. "What of the King has he caught this illness?"

Staggering away with their horses to the castle stables after releasing their stretchers this stable hand replied. "Yes sir; but I think you will find that Ordmin is doing his best to care for our King."

Walking through the corridors after passing several guards that were slouched over from this sickness Cretorex with his young men noticed the stench in the air from all this illness around them, which is why he said to Prince Hobart and Gettard. "My advice is we should cover our faces with rags to stop breathing in this foul air!"

As soon as they arrived at the King's chambers door Cretorex went on to say. "As soon as we have seen the King I would like you two to get as many of those people that are not suffering from this illness to set up a make shift camp for isolation outside the castle walls."

Entering into their Kings chamber after knocking upon his door, Cretorex almost tripped over one of the king's guard who was lying with pain directly behind the door.

After regaining his balance he came upon Ordmin with several of the Kings personal servants rushing about frantically trying to keep King Hagair's temperature down with cloths from bowls of cold water while he lay there helplessly sweating in his bed.

On seeing their medicine man walk into the room Ordmin said.

"Good you're back, the King was asking for you before he became delirious with this fever. Perhaps you can tell us how to control this disease?"

Walking to the side of the Kings bed Cretorex began to examine his patient as he replied. "I'll see what I can do, how long has he been like this?"

"Since yesterday; Most of the castle came down with it within these last two days."

After examining his King, Cretorex decided there was only one cure for this type of fever he would have to go into the forest to find a Branten tree that had a rare fungus which grew at a certain height in amongst its leaves.

This he could only achieve if he had someone who knew this forest and it's trees along with being a lot younger for climbing than himself, so he decided to take Fendale the gypsy with him, the only problem was that Fendale had been sent by Ordmin into the forest with Cumbart and some other students to find as much burning wood as they could so as to keep the castle fires burning.

With this in mind Cretorex left Ordmin to carry on with his nursing before he left the castle in haste to go and find Fendale.

While Cretorex was away Gettard and Prince Hobart organized with those that were still on their feet the marquees to be erected for the exterior of this castle so that the segregation of those that were well could sleep safely that night.

That afternoon Cretorex was back with his fungi, grinding it to powder with his pestle he immediately added boiling water to the fungus with other ingredients to produce the medicine he required.

Now with the right kind of medicine he quickly administered the first dose to his King followed with all those that were seriously ill.

Meanwhile Ordmin, on Cretorex's instructions, was organising the student's dormitory as an isolation unit for the sick, now with everything in order Cretorex was able to concentrate more on the Kings condition.

As the King finally became better after two days of sweating the fever out of his system it was apparent that a change had altered his personality, he started to glare uncontrollably at all those that were around him in such a manner that it looked as though he was ready to murder someone.

On the third day, sitting up in his bed, his first command was to Ordmin to have all of his guards whether they were ill or not stand in line outside in the castle court yard ready for his inspection.

An hour for dressing is what it took for the King as he managed to limp his way to the outside in his weakened state, standing there in front of thirty men he selected at random one of them to stand out in front then ordered him to strip naked in front of his comrades.

With embarrassment this man obeyed his King; Ordmin who was disturbed at his sovereign's command turned to him nervously and said. "Sire; How long has this guard got to stay here like this?"

"Until I say he can move. Ha. Ha. Ha. The rest of the men can go and jump off the turrets. Ha. Ha. Ha.

This laughter continued from the King as he ran back with his limp uncontrollably to the inside of his building leaving Ordmin there to make an excuse on his majesties behalf towards the rest of the guards.

"His highness is still delirious from his illness; we shall all endeavour to go along with his unusual behaviour until he is well again."

With the poor guard shivering with cold; Ordmin told him to dress again before instructing him for his own protection to go and disappear for the rest of the day.

After two weeks the make shift camp was dissembled outside the castle as most of the inflicted had recovered from this fever except for those few who had succumbed to mental problems including the King.

Several months passed within the castle, in that time the King became uncontrollable in his actions towards all those that came into close contact with him. He would often demand from his subordinates impossible tasks that no one found easy to fulfil so much so that his personal guards were now plotting to dethrone him.

Ordmin, who had noticed all this bad feeling, had decided to plan a way of keeping order within the castle.

He employed the services of Cretorex who was at this time on one of his rare visits to the castle.

He had him supply a sedative to be administered into the Kings wine on a daily basis.

This he did with immediate results as King Hagair was soon limping around his chambers in a stupor of not knowing what day it was or where he was.

As time went by some of the students were ready after being trained in many war scenarios for their inauguration to become Knights; Recognising this Ordmin approached the King carefully to ask him if he would agree to oversee the proceedings of Knighting some of these young men.

Now with the King's consent the day had arrived for three of these young students' named Gettard, Cumbart and Fendale who were now standing in the grand hall in front of their King for their inauguration.

This hall was crowded out with most of the inhabitants of the castle who were there on their Kings request trying to show what a good monarch he could be, little did they know it was Ordmin who had engineered this coming together as a way of keeping order within his majesty's realm.

King Hagair, now holding the large investiture sword in his hand was swaying slightly from its weight as he moved forward to individually dub the three students kneeling side by side in front of him.

"I King Hagair Victinours of the lands of Tonest declare that from this day on that you three of my subjects are to be Knights of various colours to serve, protect and conquer all that endangers my realm."

As he said this declaration his sword individually tapped their heads and shoulders the King who was holding his notes in his other hand pronounced their future titles as he proclaimed.

"Stand, Sir Gettard Endevoure, Knight of the flying Black bat!"

"Stand, Sir Cumbart Raymond, Knight of the Yellow sun ray!"

"Stand, Sir Fendale Blades, Knight of the Green forest!"

With them now Knighted, Ordmin with the crowd in the hall started to clap except for one person that was Prince Hobart who was standing alongside Ordmin behind the King; he was at this time upset at not being awarded for his services to his father.

That is why the Prince after noticing his father's illness was not getting any better was now in his brother's absence befriending as many of the castle residents as he could to bring them into his service with the prospect of them making him their King.

That is also why a year later after many relapses of the King; Ordmin, having also found out about Prince Hobart's plan told the now Knighted Gettard to go and hide the Kings crown in the canyon of Vorth so as to stop Hobart from being crowned as he knew this young boy would take the throne for himself before his brother.

Early one morning, Sir Endevoure quietly left his new chambers so as not to wake up anyone in the main building of the castle to make his way to the stables where he met Ordmin who was holding the royal crown.

Placing it into a cloth bag Ordmin said to Sir Endevoure. "When you are at the canyon of Vorth place it in one of the caves where your Bisthion lives, but make sure no one sees you do it or we will both be in trouble."

"Yes sir it will be good to see my pet again I've missed him."

"Forget about your pet just make sure you get this right?"

Tying the bag to his saddle then climbing onto his horse Sir Endevoure replied. "Yes sir I will.

Chapter Thirteen

Kidnappers

Leaving the castle well behind him, the Knight, riding his horse, made no time at all in reaching the outskirts of Vorth.

Once there Sir Endevoure called at the landowner's farm house for information on how his Bisthion's health was, at the same time he collected some fodder for his pet before setting off again.

As he made his way to the canyon his thoughts were of his pet Bisthion; was he well, was he still eating and would he still receive me as a friend, these thoughts he would have every time he visited him at any opportunity in those past years.

Sure enough on his way down the path Sir Endevoure could see him standing there now fully grown with his well shaped curved horns under a glossy black main, the colour of his muscular brown body of a lion shone in the sunlight along with his beautiful swishing tail of a bull, had at this moment in time come out of its cave after smelling the scent of his friend and master.

After riding steadily down the narrow path into this canyon, Sir Endevoure had now dismounted some distance from his pet so as not to frighten his nervous horse.

Then walking cautiously towards his Bisthion, Sir Endevoure held his hand out to stroke it, but as he came within inches of his pet the animal decided to veer away in play like a dog bouncing up and down only to stop again out of arms reach in ready for the Knight's next move.

"Come here boy, stop messing about," Our knight said as he was not in the mood for playing.

This carried on for some time until Sir Endevoure thought it best to sit down and wait for his pet to come to him, this he did with the immediate result of his Bisthion moving up towards him with its head bending down for a cuddle.

After sitting there for some time Sir Endevoure decided it was time to fetch the fodder from the back of his horse so as to keep his pet occupied by feeding him well away from the caves.

While his pet was busy munching on this hay the Knight headed towards the centre cave out of three that were there with the Kings crown, once inside the smell of animal urine was nearly unbearable for him as he stretched up to the highest point to place this crown on a ledge at the far end of this cave.

As he came back out into the daylight he had to adjust his eyes again to the brightness of the day before checking that he was not being watched.

Now satisfied that all was in its place Sir Endevoure said his goodbyes to his Bisthion before setting off again up the path then on towards the garrison for a surprise visit to see Lord Darnley and his daughter Silvianda.

About forty minutes into his ride on the outskirts of this fortress Sir Endevoure was approached by four of the garrison's hardnosed warriors who were riding fully armed in a menacing way towards him.

Seeing Sir Endevoure who was at this time dressed in ordinary clothes decided to surround him with their swords at the ready, the warrior facing him who seemed to be in charge demanded to know what this knights movements were and where he had been for the last two days.

Sir Endevoure immediately drew his own sword as a defence before saying. "It's none of your business as to what I do, stand clear and let me through or be prepared to defend yourselves."

Just as he said these words one of the warriors positioned behind him, hit the young Knight across the back of his head with the hilt of his sword knocking him unconsciously from his horse to the ground.

The next thing Sir Endevoure knew was he was in the garrison when he was awakened by a ruffian going though his clothes looking for something of value as he lay there while being imprisoned in a wooden barred compound amongst other undesirables. Grabbing this ruffian's hands Sir Endevoure pushed him away before standing up; this created a scuffle between this so called thieve as the undesirable attacked Sir Endevoure in such a way that the Knight had to retaliate with two punches to this man's head, knocking him out cold to the ground.

By this time two guards outside the compound rushed forward with their pikes and thrust them through the compound bars with their points towards Sir Endevoure pinning him to the far side of the cage.

Lucky for Sir Endevoure was that all this attention alerted one of Lord Darnley's senior men who recognised the Knight from the last time he had visited the garrison.

The senior man immediately walked over to see why the King's nephew was imprisoned in such a way when he said to Sir Endevoure. "What the hell are you doing in here?"

Having nowhere to go because of being pinned with the pikes Sir Endevoure replied. "I don't bloody know, I was confronted outside by four of Lord Darnley's idiotic henchmen, the next thing I know is being stuck in here like some common criminal."

"That's not right, I'll find out why they have done this to you?" Was the reply from the senior man before turning to his men for an answer "Who is responsible for imprisoning this man? Release him now and take those pikes away from his chest."

It did not take long for the guards to release Sir Endevoure, once out of the compound the senior man explained the reason why Lord Darnley's warriors were gathering as many suspicious looking men outside their garrison as they could, as he went on to say. "Yesterday morning Lord Darnley's daughter Silvianda went missing on one of her daily rides, her escort was distracted from her when they were unseated from their mounts as a log was swung towards them. As they got to their feet she had disappeared from view, after searching for her for most of that day without results Lord Darnley lost his temper when he told his warriors that they had his permission to round up as many suspects as they could."

As memories of his mothers kidnap come flooding back, fear along with anger for Silvianda's life was too much for Sir Endevoure, now very upset by not seeing his love again, he eventually reclaimed his horse before making his way to the manor where he explained to Lord Darnley how he was going to find Silvianda.

As he was there his Lordship presented Sir Endevoure with a set of armour that used to belong to him in the hope that it would protect the Knight in his progress of searching for his daughter.

This armour was silver in colour consisting of a white plume from the helm; its shield was painted with the crest of a castle on a hill.

After a good meal at the manor; Sir Endevoure now looked taller in his armour, he had grown in height to over seven foot as he mounted his horse again. Now with the two man escort that Silvianda had before she was kidnapped Sir Endevoure had decided to set off from the garrison before the night started to appear in the hope of seeing if they could pick up any signs of finding Silvianda.

Setting up camp for the night with no results from searching for any clues in their last hour of looking, this group thought it best to wait for the morning light before continuing their search.

That night around their camp fire these two men told stories of their past experiences, mostly of their adventures that they had from their early years of fighting for Lord Darnley before the garrison was built.

Now on good terms with his fellow rider's whose names were Piarus and Marriant, Sir Endevoure led the way that next morning in full armour after finding the last known tracks from where his two companions had been knocked from their horses.

Crossing two streams along with one forest they suddenly came upon a hamlet in a clearing consisting of several wooden shacks, one monastery with cemetery and a drinking house.

As they passed the cemetery they noticed the gathering of several local residents in mourning around a recently dug grave.

Suddenly from out of the nearby drinking house other residents of this hamlet ran out shouting abuse towards the Knight and his friends.

Seeing this Sir Endevoure took his sword from its sheath.

"Get ready to defend yourselves?" He said to his men as the unruly crowd was about to come to blows with the Knight and his companions.

That is when a voice shouted out from over where the mourners were at the cemetery. "Stop, hold your ground." These men are friends; their shields display the crest of Lord Darnley our protector."

Now surrounded by the occupants of this community the Knight with his companions explained to the head man why they had encroached upon his hamlet.

It was after their explanation of trying to locate the whereabouts of Silvianda that the truth was told of why this community had reacted so aggressively towards them. The head man explained, "Four days ago a Knight with several men fully armed had attacked our settlement for no reason. When we retaliated against them we lost and they made an example of us by hanging four of our young men as well as taking these men's wives as hostages."

As soon as Lord Endevoure heard that a Knight was involved it sent alarm bells ringing. He thought. "Was this Drago the Red Knight?"

Responding to the head mans story Lord Endevoure asked. "Did this Knight have a red plume on his helm and did his shield bare the sign of the red dragon?"

"He did, why, do you know him?" "Yes we do, in what direction did they go when they left here?" Pointing towards two different directions of the sea and the garrison this head man replied. "The men who captured our women headed towards the sea but that Knight set off by himself in the other direction."

Lord Endevoure thanked the head man for his information as he now realised that Silvianda was taken from the garrison after the confrontation at this hamlet.

That is when he made a promise to the head man that they would do all they could to bring back their women.

Chapter Fourteen

Pursuers of Men

While riding some distance from the hamlet within the same forest these three hunters observed signs of a struggle in an area of thick undergrowth, on closer inspection Piarus after dismounting discovered the remains of a female's clothing that seemed to have been ripped from its owner's body.

Peering further into the undergrowth Piarus pointed as he said. "It looks like a rape has taken place here the grass has also been flattened towards that direction."

Looking worried Sir Endevoure replied. "Go have a look, but be careful you never know it might be an ambush."

Two minutes had passed when Piarus reappeared with his head lowered in distress at what he had just found in this long grass.

"Well what did you find?" The Knight asked.

"It's not good, you can see for yourself." Piarus replied.

Now off their horses Sir Endevoure with Marriant were overcome with horror as they discovered the mutilated naked body of one of the hamlet's women, her flesh stripped in places by knife wounds from a frenzied attack was now laying face down from being thrown at some distance from where she was originally murdered.

Fearing for Silvianda's life along with the other women Sir Endevoure said. "We must hurry before these killers murder all their captors."

With the woman's body covered with bracken the three pursuers were now riding again as this forest disappeared behind them the land had began to soften underfoot for their horses that is when our Knight with his companions; decided to dismount as a precaution against their horses spraining their fetlocks.

As they began to walk the scenery dramatically changed to the form of small sand dunes. After some length of time trekking, the three searchers started to hear the sounds of crying in the far distance from behind one of the dunes.

Marriant suddenly let go the reins of his horse as he decided to run over to the dune in the hope of rescuing whoever it was crying in distress behind it.

Now out of sight of his companions Marriant suddenly gave out a desperate scream of shear pain as if being seriously wounded by whoever it was behind the dune.

Drawing their swords the Knight with Piarus started to run towards the dune as the screams turned into moans of someone dying, it was when they were able to view of the other side of the dune that they were struck with the real horror of what had just occurred. There in front of them was poor Marriant being squeezed to death by the tentacles of a giant octopus.

This octopus having twenty foot long tentacles was also six foot in height had just started to bite into Marriant's stomach for its lunch.

It was when this monster looked up that it was alerted by the Knight's presence. Sir Endevoure was startled when he was confronted with the part features of a young maiden set around the blood soaked beak of an octopus.

Piarus ran in towards it with his sword thrashing at these tentacles in the hope that his friend would still be alive, but in doing so was immediately hit in the face with such force that he flew back into the air with several suction marks down one side of his face.

It was obvious to the Knight that Marriant was already dead so he sheathed his sword then walked back calmly to his horse, mounted it, took his lance from its holster, lifted his shield to his side, then with a jab from his heels charged his horse forward towards his prey.

Octopus and steel do not mix as this lance from Sir Endevoure found its mark when it eventually succeeded in piercing the centre of the octopus's fleshy body.

As blue ink stained the sand after oozing out of its body Sir Endevoure was knocked from his horse by one of the octopus's tentacles as the beast started to go into a spasmodic shock of dying.

Now on the ground the knight quickly picked himself up then with his sword as a dagger in both hands ran forward to thrust the sword up to the hilt into the eye of the octopus.

With the beast dead Sir Endevoure was amazed at how its body, that was still caressing the dead Marriant, had started to shrivel back into that of a pretty young maiden.

By this time Piarus on the ground had rolled out of harm's way when holding the side of his face as he sat there staring in shock at his friend's mutilated body.

There was no time to ponder over this death for Sir Endevoure when he turned to the sounds of more crying from behind other sand dunes that were in the near area.

Retrieving his lance before mounting his horse again the Knight furtively rode to each and every one of the sand dunes with the result of finding other young maidens who were also waiting there for their next victims.

After killing about eight of these monsters with his lance Sir Endevoure was now satisfied that they were all dead before riding back to Piarus who was at this time prizing his friend's body away from the now changed arms of this beast;

Sir Endevoure dismounted and quietly said. "After we have buried Marriant we shall ride off out of this place as soon as possible, we still have to find Silvianda and the three remaining women; it's obvious they are still alive. I have just discovered some shallow tracks of horse's hoofs along with footprints over there in the distant sand."

With Marriant buried and now travelling with the sea beside them as they rode on firmer sand, Sir Endevoure, with Piarus, started to observe in the distance the outline of their adversaries.

From their distance they were not sure as to how many men they would eventually encounter. Sir Endevoure suggested to Pirus that they should leave the beach, keep on following, then wait until the light diminishes for the evening before encircling their foe through the outlining dunes positioned to their left in the hope of a surprise attack.

After closing the distance between themselves and their enemy Sir Endevoure decided to discard his armour along with their horses at a convenient hiding place for their future collection if, or when, they would eventually return.

Now positioned out of view but in sight of their prey both hunters with only shields and their knives were now on top of one of the dunes and could see several tethered horses, behind these horses were six heavily armed men who were just about to make camp for the night.

On closer inspection the three women were sitting tied up nearby while shivering in a huddle together.

Sir Endevoure was upset at seeing there was no sign of the Red Knight or Silvianda that is when he whispered to Piarus. "We shall wait till they are asleep then we will have a better chance of a successful rescue."

Piarus replied. "Shush I agree!"

Twenty minutes later in complete darkness the Knight with his companion carrying only knives crept out from behind their sand dune to make their way down in amongst their intended victims.

Now creeping between sleeping bodies the two assailants missed the lone figure that was on guard duty on the outside of the kidnapper's camp.

With four men dead after having their throats cut the guard was alerted by the muffled groan of one of his comrades demise.

Running towards Sir Endevoure with his sword held high the guard brought it down in the hope of splitting the Knights' head in two, but was suddenly amazed at the speed of his intended victim when Sir Endevoure dodged to one side.

Now with the advantage of his knife being in the right position; Sir Endevoure thrust it forward into this guard's gut causing him to scream out loud like an animal in distress.

By this time Piarus was in a wrestling match with the last remaining man who had been alerted by his companion's scream.

The man now on top managed to disarm Piarus from his knife was also now in the process of strangling with both hands around Piarus's throat until Sir Endevoure on seeing his friend's plight threw himself forward into a dive with the result of pulling this man off with his arm around the side of the man's head.

With Sir Endevoure under the weight of the man's body, Piarus immediately picked up his knife then shoved the blade into the back of this man's nape causing an unexpected gush of blood to splatter up into his face.

While all this was going on the three women were cowered on the ground together in terror from the sight of all this violence around them.

Seeing the women Piarus picked himself up and walked towards them with his hand out in the hope of reassuring them of his friendship, the problem was that all three women screamed in fear of losing their own lives from someone with such a blooded face standing there in front of them with his knife still in his other hand.

"Do not worry I shall not harm you, we are here to take you back to your kinsmen." Piarus said as he quickly sheathed his knife so as to put these women at ease.

By this time Sir Endevoure had managed to shove the dead man off from on top of him as he now stood there staring through the darkness at the sight of their hard nights work of killing before he turned to Piarus to say. "I suppose we'll have to gather these bodies up into a pile ready for either burying or burning."

With this statement one of the women interrupted before Piarus had a chance to reply.

"Don't bother, let the bastard's rot for the crows, that's all they're good for."

The woman was soon put in her place when Piarus said.

"Just because we killed them, we are not heartless enough as to not give them a proper burial even though in your eyes you think they do not deserve it."

It did not take long for Sir Endevoure and Piarus as they dug a large shallow hole in the soft sand with their shields which they had collected from behind the sand dune.

Now with these six men buried and the success of freeing the women Sir Endevoure asked them if they had seen the Red Knight or the young Silvianda while they were travelling with their kidnappers. Pointing into the far distance they said that their captor's had mentioned that they were to meet up with this Knight at a fishing village to the east of where they were now standing.

This was good news to Sir Endevoure as he told Piarus to go back to the garrison after he had taken the women back to their hamlet because he himself had decided that they should part company so that he could carry on in the rescue of Silvianda.

Chapter Fifteen

The Assassins

With the morning light appearing after travelling some distance in full armour Sir Endevoure arrived on his horse at the outskirts of the fishing village where he cautiously dismounted before walking towards the seafront in the hope of clues to the whereabouts of the Red Knight and Silvianda.

He had only walked a short distance when he was confronted with a ball hitting his shield from some youngsters who were playing outside near of one of the cottages of this village.

Bending down after releasing his horse's reigns Sir Endevoure began to retrieve the ball for these juveniles.

With this Knight's concentration being taken from his objective he did not see the two sinister figures approach him from behind as they made their attack in the hope of a quick kill.

Lucky for Sir Endevoure was the low sun of the morning from behind these assassins was casting their shadow in front of the Knight allowing him to instinctively react by turning with his sword out of its scabbard.

As their swords just missed their mark these two unfortunate killers felt the Knight's cold steal as it sliced across their stomachs leaving both of them with serious gaping gashes that buckled their torso's to fall to the ground.

Looking down at them with his sword against one of the men's neck Sir Endevoure demanded. "Who sent you to assassinate me?"

With a painful reply this man said. "Nobody sent us."

Sir Endevoure thrust his sword through his throat, as the blood shot out he replied with the words. "Not good enough."

The other man was now shaking with fear from seeing his partner's demise as Sir Endevoure realigned his sword to his throat then asked him the same question. "Well, who sent you?"

That did the trick as the other man replied. "Just like you a Knight but with a red plum in his helm."

"Where was this Knight heading and did he have a young woman with him?"

"If I tell you, you promise you will not kill me?"

"I promise, now where did they go?"

This put this ambusher at ease when he replied while starting to cough up some blood from his stomach wound. "The Knight had the girl tied by her hands when he hired a fisherman to take them both in his boat out to sea, where they were heading I have no idea, you could ask another fisherman they might know."

With this reply Sir Endevoure lifted his sword high as this man shrieked when he uttered. "You promised." "So I lied." Replied Sir Endevoure as he swiftly brought his sword down only to cut this man's head off creating a pool of blood that shimmered on the ground in the sunlight.

By this time all the young children were standing there with their mouths open from the sight of two gruesome deaths that they had never seen before.

As Sir Endevoure regained the reigns of his horse he said to these youngsters as he passed them. "Do not worry I am not here to harm you, your ball is over there in that blood."

That did it for the youngsters as they all ran off in different directions screaming in fear of their lives.

Now at the moorings of many boats Sir Endevoure had little luck when enquiring to other seafarer's about the direction of where the fisherman had taken the Red Knight and his own love Silvianda.

After pondering over his loss for most of that day of searching in vain for an answer Sir Endevoure decided to make his way back to the garrison to report to Lord Darnley of his failure in saving his daughter.

But before making his way back to the garrison the Knight visited the hamlet to see that Piarus had safely delivered the three women back to their families.

After locating Piarus, Sir Endevoure was surprised to see that his friend had set up home with one of the women and would not be travelling back to the garrison as he had now found happiness for the first time in his life.

One day later Sir Endevoure entered through the gates of the garrison only to find Lord Darnley had deployed most of his men in the search for his daughter with no success.

This had made the Lord bitter towards life in general.

On riding towards the manor Sir Endevoure noticed the grim looks on most of the garrison's resident's, there was no cheering for his presence as he met Lord Darnley with his guards on the steps of the manor.

Dismounting from his horse the Knight was immediately barraged with questions from the Lord as this nobleman was desperately relying on the Knight's success in bringing his only child back.

"Well where is she?" "Did you find out who took my daughter?" "Why have you come back without her?" "Where is Silvianda?"

With his head down as a sign of frustration Sir Endevoure replied reluctantly. "We tried our best, but we were too late Prince Drago the Kings son has managed to escape us by taking your daughter abroad somewhere. Where, we could not find out as no one knew in a fishing village some distance from here where this Prince had set sailed to."

This was the last hope for Lord Darnley as his face turned red with rage before saying to the Knight. "Your best is not good enough, clear off I don't want to see you again until you have brought back my daughter."

Then turning to his guards the Lord said. "Make sure Sir Endevoure leaves the garrison and he is not allowed back here again until I say he can."

Walking back with his horse to the gates with two guards in tow Sir Endevoure was saddened at falling out of favour with Silvianda's father as he now began to mount his steed for his trip back to castle Tonest.

Chapter Sixteen

Jousting Knights

Several miles later on the outskirts of a large open expanse of grassland Sir Endevoure came upon, in the distance, a tethered horse alongside a large blue marquee, on nearing this shelter he noticed leaning outside a lance stuck in the ground beside a large shield along with a helm strategically placed in front with its blue plumage displayed there for all to see.

On this shield the crest of a clump of bluebells on silver back ground which suggested to Sir Endevoure that this was Sir Bellingham the Blue Knight which he had heard of in his early years at the castle.

It was rumoured that this Knight's father was a Lord with a large army who was at one time a mortal enemy of King Hagair until they reluctantly united their forces to fight off an invasion against a massive army from across the seas.

From this unification of strength the son was knighted by King Hagair to become the Blue Knight who in turn had sworn allegiance to Tonest castle in case they were ever in serious trouble again.

Feeling down-hearted and frustrated Sir Endevoure thought it would be a good idea if he was to challenge this Knight to a joust in friendly combat.

These combats were expected of Knights in times of peace to keep them in practice in case of unexpected invasions.

Taking out his lance from its holster then riding up to the Blue Knight's shield Sir Endevoure hit it with his lance with an almighty clang followed with the words of. "I, Sir Endevoure, challenge thee Sir Knight?"

As soon as the challenge was made a Knight appeared with a servant from out of the marquee, on seeing his suitor the Knight a tall dark haired man lifted his helmet from the ground and replied. "About time, I was beginning to think there were no Knights left in this realm."

Once on his horse with his lance and shield the Blue Knight pulled his visor down then rode some distance from his challenger in preparation for his return, of his attack for this joust.

Now facing each other with their lances at the ready both Knights simultaneously heeled their horses before charging towards their unmistakable targets.

On reaching each other both lances clashed against opposite shields with no effect of unseating their opponents.

With sizeable indentations in both shields the two Knights charged again from different ends with the result of both Knights being unseated from their horses as this time each shield with rider took the full force of one another's lance.

Struggling to their feet in full armour these two Knights drew their swords at the same time into double hands; twang went their swords which caused a ricochet of such force that both of Knight's arms shuddered from this intensive blow.

This sword fight went on for an hour with both Knights being well matched in their skill of swordsmanship until through complete and utter exhaustion their legs started to buckle from their continuous battle. These Knights were now kneeling opposite each other while leaning on their swords and seemed to have had enough as they breathed heavily. That is when Sir Endevoure puffed as he said after lifting his visor to his helm. "Would you yield if I was to yield at the same time?"

Sir Bellingham nodded, as he took his helmet off to cool down before he replied. "I would Sir Knight, whom have I the privilege of fighting?"

"I am the nephew of King Hagair also the son of the late Lord Endevoure; they call me Sir Endevoure. I believe you are Sir Bellingham the Blue Knight?"

Both Knights were now feeling a little sore from their encounter as Sir Bellingham replied. "Yes I am, we should try this again another day but not now. If you like, you are welcome to stay for food at my marquee, that is, if you are hungry?"

Inside the marquee the Blue Knight's man servant, a small elderly man with a grey beard, had prepared food for his master was now told that he had to serve two weary Knights instead of one as both of these warriors entered this shelter.

Now with their armour off, the two Knights sat down in deep conversation of past experiences while filling their stomachs with food and wine.

After two hours of feasting Sir Bellingham insisted that Sir Endevoure should rest up for the night, as his servant had set aside an extra area for sleeping.

During the night a sinister figure holding a knife moved furtively towards Sir Endevoure with the intention of killing him in his sleep that is until his new found friend Sir Bellingham awoke just in time to stop this happening.

Moving fast from the ground that he was laying on Sir Bellingham threw himself at the assassin before this person had a chance of harming his intended victim.

With his arm around this man's neck in a tight strangle hold Sir Bellingham was surprised when he realised who it was he was throttling, it was his man servant that he had known for most of his time of being a Knight.

Awakened by the noise of this scuffle Sir Endevoure was shocked to see his host on top of his own servant laying across his legs after knocking him out from his stifling grip.

As Sir Bellingham released this grip on his servant he stood up to retrieve the knife from the ground before saying to his guest. "It looked as though my manservant wanted to kill you, does he know you from somewhere or have you ever seen him before?"

Pushing the servant away from his legs before standing Sir Endevoure replied. "No never, just like I have never seen you before this day but know you only by reputation."

"Well I will tie him up for the night as a precaution against him doing any more harm to you then we will find out in the morning why he wanted to kill you."

The next morning when Sir Endevoure awoke from his restless sleep he noticed Sir Bellingham was already outside of his marquee. Stepping out of this shelter our Knight was shocked to see the headless body of the servant with Sir Bellingham standing there holding his blooded sword over this mutilated body.

Before Sir Endevoure was about to question his hosts motives Sir Bellingham turned then walked passed our Knight with the words. "You better go you are not welcome here anymore."

The mood of Sir Bellingham had changed he seemed to have hatred in his eyes towards our Knight.

"Why what have I done to make you this way?" Sir Endevoure said as he was now confused with the situation.

Before walking back into his marquee Sir Bellingham replied. "You better ask someone back at the castle, if you stay here any longer I will not be responsible for my actions."

Not pressing his luck against his host Sir Endevoure decided to gather his belongings along with his horse before setting off for Tonest castle.

Now with the marquee well behind him Sir Endevoure thought to himself. "That was odd, I wonder why his attitude changed, I shall have to ask Ordmin when I get back perhaps he will have the answers I am looking for.

Even though this unusual event had just happened Sir Endevoure's mind was still in turmoil over losing his love, Silviander.

Chapter Seventeen

A New King

The castle was a welcome sight for Sir Endevoure as he rode through the gates of this fortress until seeing the flags were at half mast and with nobody there to meet him that he knew except the captain from the castle guard.

As he dismounted from his horse the captain approached him with news of the Kings unexplained demise that had happened two days before his arrival.

"You are to report directly to Ordmin before you see anyone else?" This captain said then went on to say. "He is at this moment giving a lecture in the student's dormitory; you are to go there right away?"

"Right, I will do." Sir Endevoure replied while walking his horse to the castle stables.

With his horse bedded for the day Sir Endevoure made his way down the long corridor towards the student's dormitory where on entering through the door he found that Ordmin had just finished his lecture.

Taking the Knight to one side Ordmin quietly said to him. "Nice to see you again Gettard, did you succeed in hiding the object that you were instructed to do?"

"Yes I did Sir, it is well hidden no one will find it now."

"Good, only now that the King has suddenly died what I thought would happen has happened, that usurper son of his has taken the throne for himself before waiting for his brother to come back."

"How did he manage that, what happened to the King's personal guard, did those guards not try to stop him?"

Making sure no one could hear him Ordmin replied. "No Gettard he befriended most of them with promises of making them wealthy once they had made him their sovereign, he even threatened the students along with the newly appointed Knights that if they did not support him he would make sure something bad would happen to them."

"Does he know that I have hidden the crown?"

"No he thinks the King hid it before he died, that is why I told the captain to send you to me first to warn you against anything Hobart might say to you. I suggest for your own safety that for the time being you should try and make this new King your friend."

After this warning from Ordmin, Sir Endevoure after cleaning himself with a change of clothes from his heavy armour made his way to the main hall to report to his new King with the news of his brother's antics which included the abduction of Silvianda.

At the doors of the main hall the two guards allowed Sir Endevoure to enter where he cautiously approached his new King who was sitting behind the large table to the far side of this hall.

Standing behind their sovereign was his newly appointed entourage of followers, guards and Knights.

Two of these Knights, Sir Endevoure recognised as being Sir Raymond and Sir Blades who were at this time trying to avert their eyes away from their friend because of the knowledge of their King's plans towards Sir Endevoure.

The King staring with accusing eyes towards this Knight demanded. "So you have finally returned, perhaps you can enlighten us as to where you have been these last few days?"

Sir Endevoure had to think fast, he knew any mention of the crown would seal his fate in the hands of this King so he bowed before replying. "Sire, I apologise for my absence at your time of grieving. The reason for my departure was I received a message from Lord Darnley at the garrison that his daughter Silvianda had been kidnapped."

"Ah yes that's the young damsel you fancied when we were last there, if I remember rightly my father wanted my brother as her suitor but you interfered, what have you to say about this?"

"It is true Sire that we are both attracted to one another but it is too late because your brother who has become the Red Knight has already successfully taken Silvianda away across the seas somewhere that I do not know of."

This was good news of his brother's disappearance for this usurper King, he knew the longer his brother stayed away the better it would be for him to secure his place on this throne.

The King then said to Sir Endevoure. "I warned you once about going against my father's wishes, you should have listened to me."

Turning to his guards, King Hobart gave an order. "Take him to the dungeons he can stay there until I have decided what to do with him."

As the guards approached Sir Endevoure he suddenly lunged against them with his hands into their chests knocking them backwards with the prospect of attacking his King.

Trouble was he missed the person or persons behind him when he felt a sharp pain to his head and then he felt no more.

The next thing Sir Endevoure knew was when he came round from being knocked out; there in front looking over him was Ordmin who had just been let into his cell by the dungeon guard.

"Good you are awake, how do you feel?" Ordmin said who was looking concerned at the state of his young friend.

Rubbing the back of his head Sir Endevoure replied. "I've had better days, what are you doing here?"

"I have just come from the King after pleading with him to keep you alive."

"What did that sod say then?"

"After a lot of persuasion I have got him to agree to give you a chance of your freedom, he is at this moment organizing with his men a tournament for all comers to the castle to be staged after the funeral in honour of his late father."

Now sitting up and feeling better Sir Endevoure asked. "Where do I come into this?"

"Ah well you see he has promised me that if you survive these jousts he will reinstate you as one of his Knights, as long as you swear elegance towards him."

"He has got some hope of me doing that after what he has done."

Ordmin nearly lost his temper as he grabbed his friends arm and snarled. "I suggest you lose your pride and fight for your freedom. Remember tomorrow is another day you never know what lies in the future, at least you will be alive."

"I suppose you are right".

"I know I am right, don't forget if Prince Drago was now King you would be dead already."

Sir Endevoure knew in his heart that Ordmin was right as he nodded in agreement as he commented. "When do I get released from here?"

"Three days time just before the tournament starts, do not worry I shall make sure you are well fed in here before then."

Putting his hand out to help the Knight up from the concrete floor Ordmin went on to ask. "Is there anything else you need?"

"Yes there is I meant to ask you about a Knight I met on my travels recently, I believe he is known as Sir Bellingham the Blue Knight, after a friendly joust I was asked to dine with him then after being given a cot for the night his man servant tried to kill me during that night."

"Yes I know the Knight he and his late father were allies to this kingdom, what did this servant look like?"

"He was a small elderly man with a grey beard, the problem I have is that the Knight killed this man the next morning for his attempt on trying to kill me." "Then it seemed, on information before killing his servant, he suddenly changed his attitude towards me as if he disliked me in some way."

As he stroked his beard in deep thought Ordmin suddenly remembered the earlier years before the joining of armies when there was turmoil in these lands of Tonest, which is when he replied.

"Ah that sounds like someone who had a grievance towards your father from earlier battles for power in these lands, you will just have to watch your back if you see this Knight again."

Just as Ordmin had finished talking the dungeon guard appeared to instruct Ordmin that he was needed elsewhere as the King was asking for him.

With the departure of Ordmin, Sir Endevoure had all the time in the world to make sure he was mentally ready for the days ahead.

The Knight had never been so low in all his life, he had lost his parents and his love, Silvianda, along with several prominent persons disliking him so much such as the Kings sons, Lord Darnley and now the Blue Knight.

His only consolation was that he had Ordmin on his side but even he, his friend, would have to watch his step against this devious King.

Chapter Eighteen

𝕭attle for 𝕾upremacy

The day of the tournament was here at last for Sir Endevoure as after three days of continuous exercise within his cell, he was now fitter than he had ever been in all of his life, ready for this trial of agility.

Taken from the confinement of his cell the Knight was led by two guards to the armoury where he was met by Ordmin who was standing there with two of his students.

"Good, you have arrived. We have your armour ready for you. These students will act as your squires when you arrive at your personal marquee outside the castle walls." Ordmin said as he instructed his students to start to suit up Sir Endevoure with his armour.

This suit of armour was black in tone as was the plume from its dog shaped helm that fitted neatly around the Knights head, the gauntlets were the biggest surprise of all for Sir Endevoure when he discovered the spikes protruding from each of his knuckles as an extra deterrent against his opponents' advances.

Now walking, while being supported by his newly appointed squires, Sir Endevoure followed Ordmin to the castle stables where the Knight was confronted with his charger which had been groomed, and decked in black silk livery camouflage.

After Sir Endevoure was helped to mount his horse, Ordmin presented him with his shield, which displayed a black bat in full flight on silver back ground, before saying to the Knight. "From this day on you shall be known as the Black Knight now live up to your name and do your best in this tournament."

It is well known in ancient times that a Knight dressed in black was a Knight that stood alone against all that came his way, some say an outcast but with this in mind Sir Endevoure replied. "I will. I shall make sure that I will not disappoint you."

After saying this, his squires lifted the long heavy jousting lance into the Knights' arm.

It was not long after this Sir Endevoure was led out on his horse by his squires from the castle towards his marquee that was positioned with other marquees at the far ends of four lanes of jousting runs.

With his visor up the morning sun hit the Knights' face with so much brightness he momentarily had a job see after the darkness of those three days in the dungeons.

His eyes adjusted quickly to the sight of the occasion as he was now seeing the stands running along against the castle walls full to the brim with spectators who were cheering as loud as they could in expectation of what they were about to experience.

Suitably placed to the centre of these stands was the royal area where the King sat looking safe with his entourage around him.

As Sir Endevoure rode towards his marquee he noticed at least thirty other marquees displaying their crests on standards belonging to other Knights who had entered into this tournament.

Most of the Knights Sir Endevoure recognized as comrades in arms from previous encounters but one stood out the most as not as friendly as first thought and that was Sir Bellingham, the Blue Knight.

The Knights on their horses were now ordered by the Kings' organizer, who happened to be Ordmin, to parade in front of the royal area so as to let the King say a few words of instruction.

As they all sat there in a line with their lances lifted vertically to the skies this unruly King raised his voice as he began his domineering speech. "You are all here today to do battle against one another in the form of jousting in the lanes allotted to you as soon as my judge has allowed you all to draw your names from his helmet."

The King paused a little then went on to say. "From these two days duelling the winner shall become my personal Knight, now have your squire's draw your names for the first round and good luck."

A personal Knight to the King was a great honour, he would become the last line of defence for his monarch to stand with him in times of war; he would also be privileged to the same food as his King along with new chambers positioned next to the Kings chambers.

This King knew he had upped the ante for these Knights in the knowledge that if they were to win they would be set up for life, for most of them would now have to put their best efforts into these jousts especially as these heats would take them at least two days to complete because each Knight would have to fight losers as well as winners.

The idea being that the Knight with the most wins out of at least twenty nine fights would be the ultimate winner of this tournament that is if they are not seriously injured in any way.

As Sir Endevoure turned his horse around in its new livery alongside the other Knights so as to make their way back to their marquees he noticed Sir Bellingham with his visor up just staring at him with hatred in his eyes.

Trying not to let this put him off Sir Endevoure was now back at the marquee where his squires told him that he would be competing in the third double joust of the first round against Sir Larkit of Tor a renowned Knight from the west lands.

Sir Endevoure had heard of this Knight's reputation for being fair even though he had never met him, so he expected this Knight would still be up to the challenge of a clean joust.

With the first four jousts of the day out of the way with no serious injuries it was Sir Endevoure's turn for his bout as he was now sitting there ready facing his opponent at his end of the jousting lane.

Down at the far end in the lane but one to Sir Larkit was a Knight called Sir Wolfhead of the field a giant of a man who rarely took any prisoners.

Looking across to the flag to be dropped for the off Sir Endevoure noticed in the lane next to him a familiar Knight just sitting there awkwardly on his horse, this Knight was Sir Raymond the Yellow Knight who gave Sir Endevoure a cheeky wink before he pulled down his visor.

"Oh no anything could happen now with Bartram beside me." Sir Endevoure thought as he nodded in response to the wink.

With a sudden dust cloud from all sixteen hoofs after the flag had been dropped these four Knights sped forward with their lances in the horizontal position towards their designated targets.

Clang went three of these lances as they hit their opponent's shields except for Sir Raymond whose lack of attention had left his lance pointing to the ground because he had stupidly slipped to one side in his saddle and was just about holding on to his horse.

His opponent; Sir Wolfhead suddenly gave out a yell as his horse tripped over this dipped lance with the result of sending him from his saddle with a flying leap in the direction of Sir Endevoure's jousting lane, head first.

Losing his own lance on the way Sir Wolfhead now hit his head on the rump of Sir Endevoure's charger causing the poor horse to buckle under its own back legs which sent Sir Endevoure's shield flying from his arm as he was also sent with his horse into a heap on the ground, now under his horse on its side the flying bat lived up to its name as the shield of Sir Endevoure hit the back of the head of Sir Larkit after he had just passed from his challenge against Sir Endevoure.

With three Knights on the ground after Sir Larkit had fallen there was cheers along with laughter that came from the stands as the crowds watched Sir Raymond still on his horse sway from side to side until he reached to the far end of his jousting lane where he finally slid back from his saddle to the ground onto his backside with a thud.

Now with his squires helping him out from under his horse before limping back disheartened to his marquee Sir Endevoure was angry at the stupidity of Sir Raymond's antics in dismounting him he knew from now on he would make sure he would have to win all of his jousts otherwise there would be no hope of winning overall.

By the end of that day most of the Knights had completed half of their jousts after being battered and bruised except for two novice Knights who had received severe damage to their bones and were now out of this competition.

There was only one Knight that day that had won all his jousts and that was Sir Bellingham whereas Sir Endevoure had lost one from his first ride of the day.

When the King with his entourage had left to go back to their castle's safety for the night; Ordmin made sure that all the spectator's had left the stands safely before checking on Sir Endevoure.

Now at the Knight's marquee Ordmin was surprised to see Cretorex the medicine man there who had just finished strapping Sir Endevoure's ankle with leather strips as he was lying there in pain on his cot with his armour off.

"Hello what has he done now, does this mean he will not be able to compete tomorrow?" Ordmin asked, as he was still concerned for the Knight's future.

"No it's only a sprain he should be fine by the morning as long as he keeps this support on for the night." Cretorex replied as he gathered his bag of medicines before leaving.

Lifting himself from his cot with the support of his squires Sir Endevoure said to Ordmin. "Don't you worry I still have to fight Sir Bellingham, you never know I might find out tomorrow what is troubling that Knight after our joust."

Stroking his beard in thought Ordmin remarked. "Oh about that; I have been making some enquiries and have found out that your father on the late Kings orders was responsible for the deaths of Sir Bellingham's man-servant's family all those years ago before this castle was built."

"So that's what it is about but why has he taken this so personal?" Sir Endevoure replied as he was now moving about and feeling a lot better.

"Because his servant's daughter a young girl at that time was killed as well, and that is why he has taken it so personal because that girl was a very close friend of Sir Bellingham when he was a lad."

"Why did he kill his man servant then?"

"That is something you will have to find out for yourself."

Now that Sir Endevoure had the truth of what was troubling his opponent he knew there would be no way he could make amends for his own fathers short comings, he thought he would now just have to concentrate on tomorrows jousts.

Early morning after a good night's sleep Sir Endevoure was awakened by his squires to the sound of other Knights making ready for their second big day of jousting.

Outside his marquee he could hear the fanfare as the King arrived to be seated in his area of the stands.

Sir Endevoure knew that this day would be the last chance he would have of making amends to the King and certain Knights.

After his squires help Sir Endevoure was now outside his marquee and on his horse again in ready for the days jousting, his ankle was a lot better from its nights rest.

After several Knights had completed their first jousts of the day it was now Sir Endevoure's turn as he sat there in readiness against his opponent who happened to be an old friend of his; Sir Blades the Green Knight, another prodigy of Ordmin's class of students.

With the flag dropping these two Knights with their lances charged towards each other at such speed that when they eventually met their shields shuddered from their lance's impact with no result of unseating either Knight.

On their second run towards each other Sir Blades made a small mistake in keeping his shield slightly low, in seeing this Sir Endevoure took this opportunity to aim his lance towards the armoured arm of his opponent with the result of sending Sir Blade's flying from his saddle.

Now on the ground this Knight struggled to his feet then lifted his hand up as a gesture to say he was not injured to Sir Endevoure who was now back at his end of his jousting lane.

As the day progressed there were many jousts like this with no serious injuries until the joust between Sir Raymond and Sir Bellingham, for some reason in this joust Sir Bellingham deliberately aimed his lance in the direction of Sir Raymond's neck, as it thudded against his chin guard it sent this Knight into twist to one side of his saddle, then as he rode on a little distance down his jousting lane he finally fell from his horse to the ground in a comatose state from the sudden jolt to his head.

As two stewards raced to Sir Raymond's aid with a wooden stretcher, it was then that Sir Endevoure had the inclination that Sir Bellingham had acted deliberately ruthless against this Knight because he had realised that Sir Raymond was a castle comrade of Sir Endevoure's.

After this incident time seemed to go quickly on this day for these Knights as most of their jousts were completed in record time.

Now the joust Ordmin and his King had been waiting for was about to happen as the King sat there looking at Sir Endevoure on his horse in readiness to do battle against Sir Bellingham.

Both knights had successfully won every joust that day but that still left Sir Bellingham in front from winning all his jousts on the day before.

As the flag dropped, both Knights spurred their horses at the same time. Before the encounter of both lances smashing against their shields which sent them into splintered pieces from the ferocity of their charge.

When both Knights had reached the end of their jousting lanes the squires were there to replace the lances before turning their horses for their second run.

After jousting for at least six times with four wasted lances it seemed that this battle was not going to end until on the seventh run Sir Endevoure managed with a bit of luck to aim his lance to the inside of Sir Bellingham's shield with the result of hitting him squarely in his breast plate with such force that he could do nothing but fly from his saddle into the air until he reached the ground on his back in a cloud of dust.

"At last" Sir Endevoure thought as he lifted his lance to the heavens as a salute to his King and the crowd's cheers before riding back to his marquee.

As the day progressed with the evening approaching was when the very last joust had just been run, that is when Ordmin instructed all the competitors to stand before their King to receive their rewards for their efforts of the last two days of jousting.

That day was a proud day for many of these Knights as the King came out of the stands with his guards behind him to give out titles to those that deserved them; it was until he eventually reached the last two winners as they stood there out of their amour.

"After a difficult decision I have decided Sir Bellingham will be my personal Knight but you my cousin Sir Endevoure shall become protector of the realm and you will in future report to Ordmin for any instructions that I see fit for you to perform."

Protector of the realm was a dangerous title to have as the King knew when he bestowed it upon Sir Endevoure; this Knight would always be the first line of defence in all conflicts protecting the castle which included travelling around the lands of Tonest to keep order.

To Sir Endevoure this was a worry but also good in the fact that he would be away most of the time from this King that he despised so much.

Bowing to their King before all the Knights left, Sir Endevoure noticed a silly smirk on the face of Sir Bellingham, from this look our Knight of the realm realised that the hate was still there and whatever amends he would try to do would never be enough.

Chapter Nineteen

Seeds of Evil

Over the next six months Sir Endevoure was still grieving at the loss of his love so much so that he had become bitter towards life in general, he did on several occasions kill unnecessarily to relieve himself of these frustrations, because of this he had started to gain a bad reputation amongst the villages in and around the districts of Tonest as being a Knight that was to be avoided at any given moment of contact in his job as protector of the Kings realms.

It was one day on completing a mission that Sir Endevoure was riding in full armour along a narrow track around the outskirts of a forest on his way back to the castle when he noticed ahead of him four bandits attacking an old man and a young girl who were trying desperately to get their horse to pull their cart out of thick mud.

Whether these ruffians were there to steal or not was beside the point for our Knight as he sped his horse into a gallop in the hope of rescuing this vulnerable couple from serious harm.

With his sword now out of its scabbard, Sir Endevoure sliced his metal blade through two of these bandits who were positioned on either side of his horse as he finally reached them, at the same time the other two had already knifed the old man and were in the process of pilfering through his clothes after knocking the young girl to the ground from the cart.

The old man was still alive and decided to fight back at one of these bandits only to find it was a bad idea as this attacker lifted his knife again to finish the old man off until our Knight intervened when he managed to get there just in time to send his sword through this man's body killing him instantly.

Seeing these deaths to his friends the forth bandit thought it best to run when he jumped from the cart only to find he was not quick enough because the young girl decided to stick her leg out while she was still lying on the ground sending this bandit head first into a tree to the side of the track with the result of knocking him out.

Dismounting from his horse Sir Endevoure sheathed his sword before helping the young girl to her feet when he said to her. "Have you any injuries to yourself?"

This good looking girl with long blond hair in plaits down to her waist replied. "No sir but my husband needs tending to; he does not look too well."

Leading her to the cart our Knight helped the young girl in making her husband comfortable as his wound was only superficial and only required a clean rag to stop it bleeding.

While they were tending to the old man the bandit that collided with the tree suddenly awoke from his comatose state and decided to make a run for it.

That is when Sir Endevoure turned to run after him until the young girl stopped him jumping from the cart when she said. "Let him go, I don't think he will be bothering us again especially now that you are here to protect us."

It must have been the way that the girl spoke with such a soft voice or the fact that Sir Endevoure was curious as to why a young girl had married such an older person than herself that made him decide that day to escort them both back to their cottage instead of chasing after the last bandit.

With his horse tied to the back of the cart carrying the old man a small grey haired fellow with a tiny beard, Sir Endevoure was now sitting beside this young girl in the front of the cart while holding the reigns to this girl's carthorse when he asked her. "What are yourself and your husband's names?"

"His name is Fredal and my name is Muriel." She replied.

As soon as our Knight had introduced himself to this girl she began to chatter nonstop while feeling more relaxed in his company which did not go unnoticed by her husband as he lay there behind in the back of the cart.

Half an hour later outside old Fredal's cottage Sir Endevoure helped Muriel to carry her husband from the cart to the inside of his dwelling where the old fellow asked our Knight if he would like to stay for a meal.

After accepting the invitation Sir Endevoure sat drinking mead with Fredal while his wife prepared their meal in the next room which gave the old man time to put a proposition towards our Knight when he said. "I can see my wife has taken a liking towards you so I would like to ask you a very big favour."

Curious to see what this old man had in mind Sir Endevoure replied. "What favour is that then?"

"Well you see I am now too old to give my wife children and I thought you would be the perfect man to help me achieve this problem for keeping my family's name alive for the foreseeable future."

Sir Endevoure choked on his mead at the thought of this scenario of becoming a stud for this old man before he managed to say. "How do you know that your wife would agree to your suggestion and why did you marry such a young girl in the first place if you knew that you would be incapable of starting a family?"

"That is because when we were first married I was just as young as you but after several years of being together I started to age rapidly so much so that now I am unable to perform for her. All I can say is that I must have some sort of ageing problem with my body."

"I am sorry I cannot help you, as a Knight for the King I am not here to bed every young woman that happens to come my way that would be immoral, anyway I am sure there are other suitable young men out there for her that would be only too willing to help."

"There is but like I said she has taken a liking towards you, are you sure I cannot change your mind."

Now feeling uncomfortable our Knight stood from his seat and replied. "No you can't change my mind; I think I had better go."

Just as our Knight was about to walk to the door, Muriel came into the room holding the plates with food. "Oh you are not going are you, what has my husband been saying to you? Don't take any notice of him. You must stay and eat first before riding off."

Sir Endevoure could not refuse the young girls offer as she had made such a lovely job of preparing this food that was now making his mouth water from just looking at it. "I'll just stay for the meal but then I must go." Our Knight said as he sat down again.

While eating Sir Endevoure was given another tankard of mead from his host which after a period of time started to make him drowsy before sending him forward in his seat with his head down into a shallow sleep.

Haziness accompanied with movement filled our Knights eyes as he was aware that he was not in control of the environment around him after realising that time was irrelevant as he was now in the prone position with the form of a body being there several times upon him.

Awakening from this unusual experience Sir Endevoure found himself tied by the wrists and the ankles with twine as well as being naked on a cot with the bare minimum of sheeting to protect his modesty.

As he lay there Muriel appeared carrying his under garments along with his armour within this side room of the cottage.

Placing his belongings by the side of the cot this young girl said. "You should never have come here; because of my lust of human intimacy that I am unable to control, you have become just another one of my conquests."

Now fully aware of his surrounding Sir Endevoure started to struggle with his bindings to no avail as he replied. "Why are you doing this to me, cut me loose now and where is your husband, I'll kill him if I get my hands on him."

"That would be a waste of your time as he has already been dead these last two days and is now buried outside with my other husbands who have all failed in giving me a child that I desperately wanted."

"But you must have known that when you married him the chances of him giving you a child were not good as he was too old for you. Anyway how many husbands are there in the ground outside there that you have buried?"

"I must admit I have lost count as they do not live that long after they have consummated their marriage to me."

Still struggling to get free Sir Endevoure was starting to realise that this young girl had an ageing affect on all those men that became intimate with her, which is when he decided he was now going to use a more psychological approach to her for getting himself free when he said. "How long will you keep me tied up?"

"Until you become too weak with age or until you have succeeded in becoming a father, then and only then will I free you?"

"Perhaps it is you that is incapable of having children, have you thought that this is your problem and not your partners."

As soon as our Knight suggested that Muriel was not up to the challenge she went into a ferocious rage when she suddenly grabbed the side of the Knight's cot and lifted it before sending this cot into the upside down position while screaming as loud as she could.

It was then Sir Endevoure realised that this girl was not as weak as she looked after finding himself looking at the floor in the upside down position with the feet of Muriel pounding against the underside of this cot from her unexpected tantrum.

Lucky for our Knight was that now in this awkward position his twines loosened to his wrists allowing him to release himself just before seeing the back of Muriel's legs leaving the room after calming down from her uncontrollable outburst.

Sir Endevoure still had a problem of trying to reach his ankles, failing this he pushed as hard as he could with his hands against the floor in an attempt to move the cot in to the upright position.

After what seemed like an eternity from all this movement the twines to our Knights ankles finally gave way to allow him to crawl from underneath his imprisonment where he quickly clothed himself in his under garments before rushing to the room's door with his sword in his hand.

In the next room there was no sign of Muriel she had left the cottage before Sir Endevoure had time to catch her in the event of finding out if she had infected him in any way from this ageing process.

With no sign of Muriel our Knight while searching around the outside perimeter of the cottage discovered a freshly dug grave and at least twenty mounds of earth in the form of other graves at the rear of this building, now on his knees he began scooping away with his hands the earth on this new grave only to discover that Muriel was telling the truth about her husband, there in front of him laying there peacefully with his face up was the old man Fredal.

It was while pulling the earth to one side that Sir Endevoure noticed the ageing affect had already began to take hold of him as his hands were beginning to wrinkle and also he was starting to breathe more heavily from the effort of digging.

With this in mind he decided that there was only one person in this world who could help him conquer this illness and that would be Cretorex the medicine man who he knew was at this time somewhere treating people in and around the areas of Tonest.

After finding his horse tethered nearby Sir Endevoure left his armour inside the cottage for another day when he would be strong enough to wear it again as he was now feeling very weak from this sickness that was rapidly taking a hold on him.

It must have been more than two hours when our Knight slumped over his horse finally found Cretorex who was near some cottages adjacent to grass lands while tending to some sick animals for a local land owner.

As his horse approached the healer, Sir Endevoure slipped from his saddle to the ground in front where Cretorex on seeing this was shocked at how our Knight had aged before saying. "What has happened to you? You look dreadful; here let me give you a hand before you pass out."

Lifting Sir Endevoure to his feet, Cretorex through previous experiences realised when seeing him the problem that our Knight had been through before turning to the land owner and asking him if he would supply a horse and cart for transporting Sir Endevoure back to his own dwelling where he had the medicines to treat this type of infliction.

Now with Sir Endevoure lying in the back of this cart Cretorex reined the horse to go fast in the hope of getting our Knight the treatment he needed at his log cabin on the far side of Tonest forest.

Half an hour later arriving at his cabin beside a river Cretorex hastily lifted our Knight inside where he administered to him while laying on his own cot the right potions for this type of ageing.

By this time our Knight had aged almost twenty years as his hair was beginning to thin along with many lines on his face that was making it impossible to think that he would ever be young again.

Through his years of delving into unusual events this medicine mans' knowledge was unsurpassed by anyone else in these lands from his dealings before with other beings that had the infamous gift of ageing being bestowed on all the unexpected victims that came their way.

It must have been at least two weeks of sweating this disease out of his system before Sir Endevoure's body started to reverse this ageing process along with him gaining his strength back to allow him to sit up without help.

Now feeling a lot better our Knight was ready to go back to Muriel for revenge but the only problem he had was Cretorex was not allowing him get up until he had fully recovered from this disease being out of his system as he said to him. "If you leave now you will stay at the age that my potions started to repair your body but if you stay for another two weeks for the full treatment you should be back to your normal age of before you were first affected."

Deep down Sir Endevoure knew that Cretorex was right in what he said after feeling that his medicines were helping him breathe a lot better when moving about as he replied. "All right I will give it two more weeks but no later than that as I have to retrieve my armour from that evil bitch's cottage."

Sure enough two weeks later Sir Endevoure now back to his normal self thanked Cretorex for all that he had done before setting off on his horse towards Muriel's cottage in the hope of retribution against her.

After two hours of riding without seeing anyone our Knight was in sight of this cottage, as he dismounted he crept towards the cottage door before opening it quietly to reveal Muriel sitting there in a seat with a large tummy as a result of being pregnant.

Surprised to see her like this Sir Endevoure said. "That cannot be my child it has only been four weeks since I was last here."

Ready to stand against our Knights' intrusive entrance Muriel replied. "Oh yes it is this ageing process has its own advantages too, your child should come into the world in about a week's time, you can stay here if you want to see it being born."

"No you don't, you are not using this pregnancy to keep me here, and anyway I should kill you where you stand for what you did to me, the only thing stopping me now is that you are expecting this child. So stay where you are as I have only come for my armour and I do not want to see you ever again."

"If that's the way you want it so be it, your armour is where I left it for you in the other room." Muriel said as she decided to stay in her seat because she knew that Sir Endevoure was so angry with her and that he would use any excuse he could of finding a way of getting his own back on her.

Before leaving with his armour our Knight gave a last warning to Muriel when he said. "This child you are carrying I want nothing to do with it, so if it is a boy or a girl and I come across it when it is older after finding out it belongs to you I shall kill it do I make myself clear."

"Yes perfectly clear but if you do kill this child you would be destroying your future."

Sir Endevoure just shrugged his shoulders as he replied before leaving. "That is your problem."

Outside walking to the forest with his armour in his arms along with his horse in tow Sir Endevoure suited himself up between the trees in readiness for making his way back to the castle.

Chapter Twenty

Knights Revenge

Several years passed for Sir Endevoure within the realm of Tonest, in all that time he was reluctantly sent on many quests for his King knowing that if he refused to obey his sovereign he would expect to lose his life some day from one of the Kings henchmen.

The other problem this Knight had he realised that if he was to move from this realm to live somewhere else the King would keep on sending assassins to kill him until they were successful in terminating his life.

With all these burdens being a held over him Sir Endevoure was lucky to have at least one friend within the castle, his mentor Ordmin, who on many occasions would warn our Knight of any unruly event coming his way.

Then the inevitable happened' the King suddenly had word from his spies that his brother Prince Drago and a small band of followers had landed back in his realm in the hope of reclaiming his throne.

In a bid to stop this happening King Hobart sent Sir Endevoure with twenty of his guard from the castle with the intention of annihilating this force of aggression towards him.

Little did the King know that over at the garrison Lord Darnley had word that Silvianda had come back with Prince Drago so he, with forty of his warriors, was also on his way towards this force in the hope of rescuing his daughter.

It was at a valley being overlooked by two hills on either side of its half a mile length that Prince Drago and his men under the ensign of the Red Dragon were riding in front of a carriage carrying Silvianda.

This is when, on one of those hills, Lord Darnley arrived just in time with his warriors to see Sir Endevoure with his force of guards laying in wait on the opposite hill with the prospect of ambushing this Prince.

Fearing for his daughter's life Lord Darnley positioned his archers in the direction of the Sir Endevoure's guard then with his command to his warriors they sent a rally of arrows across the valley in the hope of stopping this ambush.

To Lord Darnley this act of aggression towards the King's guard meant little to him because his daughter's life was more important than life itself, he would, if he could, do anything for her no matter what, even if it meant that when the King found out of his attack against his guards the King might take it upon himself to retaliate against the garrison.

With sheer luck Sir Endevoure sitting on his horse decided to stay behind his men when two thirds of the Kings guard were either killed or wounded as the arrows found there mark. Sir Endevoure ordered the rest of the guards to run for cover before the next volley of arrows had a chance of hitting them.

Down in the valley Prince Drago had noticed this incident above him unfold so he instructed his men to dismount from their horses and take up positions behind some rocks adjacent to the hill sides, then with his men using their long bows to let go their arrows in a counter attack against Lord Darnley's men, Prince Drago ushered the carriage with its driver through the valley using it for himself as a shield against the barrage from above.

Little did this Prince know was that Lord Darnley would never have allowed his warriors to fire upon this carriage while carrying his daughter Silvianda who was at this time cowering inside this transporter with her two year old son in fear of losing their lives from some of the stray arrows which had somehow caught the side of the carriage.

If Lord Darnley had known about this boy he would never have attacked this group in the first place but would have tried a more diplomatic solution of resolving this problem, but now that weapons had been fired against the Kings guard he was now committed with his warriors to battle on till the end.

With the carriage now out of harm's way at the very far end of this valley, Lord Darnley with half of his warriors on their horses rode off the other way towards the entrance of this valley to advance through it in a final and decisive attack, while at the same time the rest of his warriors kept Prince Drago's men pinned down behind their rocks from above with their volley of arrows.

While all this was going on in the valley the Prince with his carriage were well on their way towards the castle, after several miles through the forest of Tonest they eventually arrived in front to the closed gates of the castle.

Little did the Prince know was that Sir Endevoure with the guards had just entered the castle some time before him to enhance their numbers for a fight against Lord Darnley's warriors but when the King was informed of the arrival of Prince Drago outside his castle and also the events that had just transpired he on his orders deliberately closed these gates to protect himself from his brother taking his throne along with the threat of Lord Darnley's warriors.

Now looking down from his castle ramparts the King with his personal guard which included Sir Bellingham bellowed out as loud as he could towards his brother. "The only way to enter my castle is if you were to defeat my champion then I would stand down as King and let you take your throne otherwise you can go and get lost for all I care."

That is why this King knew that if he sent his cousin Sir Endevoure out to face up to his brother it would mean that one or both of them would lose their lives then at least he would only have one of them to contend with in the future.

Sitting there in his armour astride his horse Prince Drago replied after he had checked inside the carriage that his son was not hurt in any way. "I shall fight your champion on one condition that if I lose this fight that you will promise me that no harm shall come to my wife or child?"

The King was surprised to hear that his brother had got married let alone that he had produced an heir to his realm so of course he agreed when he said. "I promise no harm will come to either of them as long as you allow them now for their own safety to enter this castle while you fight my champion."

"I agree, now open your gates."

As the gates were opened by the castle guards, Sir Endevoure on Ordmin's orders from the King appeared in full armour upon his charger ready to do battle against his arch enemy.

At the same time the carriage was driven forward carrying its precious cargo by the only man left out of Prince Drago's followers.

As the carriage passed Sir Endevoure he noticed through his visor in his helm his lost love Silvianda holding on to her son looking really nervous at what was going to happen to her and her boy once she had entered this castle.

Seeing that she had never seen Sir Endevoure in this armour before she did not know it was him with his visor down, if she had she would have asked the driver to stop in an attempt to stop this battle.

With the carriage inside this fortress the two knights faced each other outside on their horses ready to do battle but not before Prince Drago with his shield displaying the Red Dragon said to his opponent. "Who do I have the honour of fighting this day? Come Sir Knight, show thy self."

Lifting his visor Sir Endevoure replied. "It is I your cousin Gettard the Black Knight who will today repay you for kidnapping my true love. So prepare yourself Sir Knight."

Prince Drago's mouth opened in surprise as he pulled to one side the reins of his horse to turn it he said. "So it is, let it be done."

Moving in different directions to give each other their run for their joust before turning towards each other these two Knights charged with their lances at such speed that the divots from the grass were flying everywhere in their wake from their horses hoofs.

As the Knights met in the middle of their run both men were suddenly sent flying backwards from their saddles as their lances had made contact at the same time to their shields with such force that it would have been impossible for anyone to have remained on their horses.

After struggling to pick themselves up with their shields they then quickly drew their swords from their sheaths before striking against each other's blades in a fight to the death.

This sword fight went on for ten minutes until the Red Knight managed to swipe Sir Endevoure's sword out of his hand only to find that Sir Endevoure was just as skilled with his shield as much as he was with a sword when he while using the edge of his shield left the ground in a forward dive and brought this shield around in the air to hit the Prince on the side of his helm with the result of knocking it off.

With his helmet off the Red Knight was stunned momentarily which gave Sir Endevoure time to pick his sword up then with a sudden thrust with both hands he sent his sword strait through the front of the Prince's throat causing from this fatal blow a sudden gush of blood to splatter over the Black Knights helmet.

As the Red Knight's body slumped to its knees then on his face to the ground, cheers from the ramparts could be heard from all of those watching this battle, but to Sir Endevoure there was no joy in his victory because he had began to realise that he had just killed his cousin who was supposed to have been the next King.

Chapter Twenty One

Reunion

While this battle was in progress outside in front of the castle walls, inside the driver of the carriage was killed by the Kings guards as soon as it had entered the castle that's when Silvianda was ordered out of the carriage, as she stepped out her screams from her efforts of holding on to her son were in vein as he was taken from her on the Kings orders, Silvianda was not strong enough as she tried to ward off these guards before they eventually grabbed her by the arms and marched her to the dungeons.

Back outside the castle Sir Endevoure remounted his horse and was just about to make his way back into the castle when Lord Darnley appeared from out of the forest with most of his warriors, on seeing the deceased body of Prince Drago lying there in his own pool of blood with no carriage in sight this Lord decided to ride up alone on his horse to this Black Knight.

"Sir Knight, where is my daughter? Tell me now or you will forfeit your life with my warrior's arrows."

As this Knight lifted his visor, Lord Darnley nearly fell of his horse from being surprised at seeing Sir Endevoure in this black armour.

Before this Knight could answer Ordmin appeared on a grey horse from out of the castle gates with a message from the King.

Riding towards the Lord at speed on his horse Ordmin on reaching him said. "I have been informed by the King that he is only prepared to return your daughter as long as you promise to leave with your warriors and go back to your garrison otherwise he cannot be held responsible for what might happen to you or your daughter. Well my Lord; have I a reply to give to my King?"

"You tell your King I remember him as a spoilt brat when he was running around in his bum rags with a snotty nose, and that is why, in my opinion, he is not fit to be a King, so I'll do as he asks but in the meantime if any harm has come to my daughter his words will fall on deaf ears, now you make sure he understands this or many of the people in his castle will lose their lives today."

Ordmin and Sir Endevoure found it hard not to laugh at this definition of their King as Ordmin replied. "I shall tell him my Lord but I'll try to be more diplomatic I would not like to be around him if I told him exactly what you have just said."

"I don't care how you put it to him as long as he gets the message." Lord Darnley said while lifting his arm as a signal.

With this signal just as this Lord had finished his sentence a great noise from everywhere out of the trees from around the whole perimeter of this castle appeared two hundred men after making their way from the garrison to support Lord Darnley's warriors in their bid to storm this castle.

As Ordmin turned his horse to make his way back to the castle, Sir Endevoure remarked to Lord Darnley. "If you would allow me I shall go and fetch Silvianda from the castle for you?"

"If you manage to bring her back safely then all is forgiven, you will then be welcomed back at the garrison at any time you like."

With this promise from Lord Darnley the Knight dug his heels in on his charger to race after Ordmin where he finally managed to catch up with him just outside the castle walls.

Before entering through the gates of this fortress our Knight said to his friend. "You must let me try to persuade the King to release Silvianda before you upset him with Lord Darnley's message."

Riding across the drawbridge Ordmin replied. "I will give you a chance but if it looks like the King is adamant in keeping Silvianda prisoner then we will have to plan, at a later date, a way of helping her to escape."

Now inside the castle as both men dismounted Sir Endevoure said. "Fair enough we'll see how it goes but don't hold your breath."

Sir Endevoure as well as Ordmin need not have worried because by this time the King after looking down from up on top of the ramparts automatically choked when he saw this force of Lord Darnley's men facing him had suddenly decided to order his guards to go and fetch a horse for Silvianda before releasing her from the dungeons.

Now out of her internment and in the castle yard Silvianda pleaded for her son to be returned to her with no result as the King insisted that this child was the next heir to the throne as the boy was his brother's child and had no right being brought up at the garrison.

With two guards lifting Silvianda on to the horse, one of these stupid men slapped the horse's rump which sent the animal at full speed towards the castle gates.

As sheer luck would have it Sir Endevoure had just dismounted, when he, out of the corner of his eye, noticed Silvianda holding on to the horse's main in fear of being thrown from her steed, that was when he stood in the way with his arms up in the air in front of the horse causing it to come to an abrupt halt.

Now, with the sudden stop of the horse, her body lurched forward with her arms around the neck of this skittish beast. It was then Silvianda realised who this hero of a Black Knight was, seeing it was Sir Endevoure she blurted out. "Oh it is you Gettard. I thought I would never see you again."

Grabbing the horse by the ear Sir Endevoure replied to her. "As did I when Prince Drago kidnapped you all those years ago."

"You have got to help me Gettard? The King has taken my son and he will not give him back to me."

"You have a child? Is this boy Prince Drago's son?"

"He is but it is a long story I cannot explain to you now, please you must help me"

By this time Ordmin who had been watching decided to bring Sir Endevoure's horse back to him and said. "You must get Silvianda out of here or her father will start a war if she is not returned to him soon."

Letting go of Silvianda's horse's ear then allowing Ordmin to give him a leg up on his charger Sir Endevoure replied to Silvianda. "Yes Ordmin is right we must get you out of here before the King changes his mind; when you are safe let me come back here at a later date to try and persuade the King to let you have your son back."

Even though her heart was breaking from losing her son Silvianda knew deep down Ordmin was right about her father's tenacity on getting back what was rightfully his.

With Silvianda still sobbing Sir Endevoure rode with her through the open the gates of the castle towards her impatient father.

While these two were riding towards her father enormous cheers were heard from all of Lord Darnley's men which seemed to really annoy King Hobart as he was now furious that Sir Endevoure had taken sides in this matter.

Now alongside her father Lord Darnley, his first words to her were. "Goodness you have grown into a beautiful woman!"

It was then while sitting there on their horses the Lord sided up to Silvianda's horse before leaning over in front of Sir Endevoure and gave his daughter a long awaited hug.

Chapter Twenty Two

Adoption of a prince

With the withdrawal of Lord Darnley's army the castle of Tonest seemed to be back to normal if it was not for King Hobart who was still scheming to hold on to his throne on this day after the siege when he summoned Ordmin before him.

Now standing in front of his King at the long table in the grand hall Ordmin after bowing said to his majesty. "Yes, your highness, you called for me?"

The King behind this table was sitting looking over some parchment with Sir Bellingham and lifted his hand as a gesture to Ordmin to wait until he had finished what he was doing.

Then after what seemed to be forever for Ordmin the King replied. "I have a delicate errand for you to perform for me, you are to collect my brother's son with his carer then with Sir Bellingham as an escort you are to take this child along with this woman to the forests of Rayen where you will deliver him to a woodsman who is the husband of this woman. This task is to be our secret only ourselves are to know about this, is that clear?"

To Ordmin this was a typical act of what this King was like when he asked him out of curiosity. "Yes Sire does Sir Bellingham know the way to this land of Rayen?"

The Kings face turned slightly red as he raised his voice in annoyance of being asked such a question. "Well of course he does we have just this minute worked out the route that you should both take, anyhow the carer of the boy lives there, now get on with it."

"Yes your highness."

Even though Ordmin had never been on a quest before with this Knight he was still apprehensive of how he would get on with him as Sir Bellingham was only ten years younger than himself being that he was one of the oldest Knight's in this castle, he was Knighted by the late King Hagair.

Leaving their King before walking down the corridor towards the carer's chamber Ordmin said to Sir Bellingham. "When we pick this child up I do not want you to have anything to do with him, you are only here to escort us all, so no roughness towards this boy."

Sir Bellingham gave a cough of indifference before he replied. "Don't worry the sooner we deliver him the sooner I can get back to normality from this boring task of babysitting you and this boy."

To Ordmin if he had his way he would take this boy straight back to his mother at the garrison if it was not for having this Knight accompanying them as an escort.

After introducing themselves to this woman they found out her name was Ellisher, her hair being grey showed she was well aged along with her looks of a woman that had toiled for a living for most of her life.

After collecting the boy with Ellisher it was obvious this young fellow was looking a little nervous as he started to shake as he held both hands in between Ellisher and Ordmin while walking alongside Sir Bellingham in the rain towards the castle stables for their horses.

With this boy sitting in the saddle in front of Ordmin on his grey horse alongside Ellisher's horse, Sir Bellingham was of cause in front leading the way on his mount as they were now well on their journey away from the castle towards the lands of Rayen and its forests.

After leaving the forest of Tonest the riders climbed a hill to the top and, with it still raining, they decided it would be safer for their horse's fetlocks to dismount because of the uneven track that they had noticed was there on the way down to the other side.

Now back on flat muddy ground these three riders rode on for some time until eventually they could see in the distance the edges of Rayen forests with its tall trees standing out in the skyline.

It was then that Sir Bellingham turned in his saddle and said to Ordmin. "Once we enter this forest it is up to the boy's carer to show us where her log cabin is."

It must have been half an hour before these travellers found the wooden cabin. As they rode up to the cabin Ordmin could see there was nothing special about this wooden structure but a basic square looking barn as he commented to Ellisher. "You actually live here?"

"Yes I do, but you will find it very comfortable inside." Ellisher said as she dismounted from her horse before lifting the young boy from the front of Ordmin's horse.

"If you say so." Ordmin replied having doubts that a place this small would never be comfortable.

"I do say so! You must come inside and see for yourself. Anyway I expect my husband will be inside with a warm fire to dry us all off from this rain."

Sure enough once these four were inside, this cabin's furnishings were opulent consisting of carved wooden furniture covered in most places with homemade fabrics, such as cushions, tablecloths, large rugs and curtains.

Within this comfortable environment was Ellisher's husband who happened to be sitting there in front of a roaring fire, not being able to work in the forest this day.

Being of medium height with broad shoulders that were covered with long ginger hair over his snubbed nose under very light blue eyes which were outshone by his rugged red complexion from working outside all of his life.

Seeing that he was a forester this man had large blisters on his hands as he greeted Ordmin with a strong hand shake after he had reluctantly found the strength to rise from his seat after dozing in the warmth.

"Welcome!" he said, then went on to say after kissing his wife on the cheek. "Is this the young fellow who is to be an addition to our family?"

"He is. See that you treat him well, he is very special boy. Have you thought of a name for this child?" Ordmin replied as he was a little concerned for the boy's safety.

"We have!" Replied Ellisher before her husband could answer.

She then sat the young boy down on a chair to dry him off with a large cloth.

"He will now be known as "Ixor" the forester's son."

"Well that's settled then we might as well go now that we have completed our errand." Sir Bellingham said while trying to be patient because he just wanted to get back to the castle.

But before Ordmin and the Knight had a chance to leave, Ellisher insisted that they should eat before their journey back.

After a very good meal the newly named boy called Ixor spoke for the very first time in the presence of his new formed family when he asked. "Mummy my mummy?"

Ordmin decided to reply to the awkward question when he said. "One day soon but in the meantime you will have to stay here with these people as your new family until your mother returns again."

Ixor was then taken by Ellisher to his area in the cabin where his cot was, then talking to him softly while sitting on the edge of this cot Ixor slowly dropped off to sleep.

It was late afternoon for Ordmin riding together with Sir Bellingham finally found their way from the cabin out of Rayen forest.

With the rain easing off these two riders now found it a lot easier as they sped onwards on their horses towards castle Tonest.

Chapter Twenty Three

Internment

When arriving back at the garrison after travelling, Lord Darnley and his warriors, along with our Knight, Sir Endevoure, found it hard to console Silviander after the loss of her son as she was now heartbroken thinking that she would never see him again.

Back inside the Manor house with her father, Silvianda over a period of time started to kindle her love again for Sir Endevoure as he was now living nearby in one of the rooms of this building.

After long talks with Silvianda, Sir Endevoure established how she survived all those years away from her own environment. She explained to him that Prince Drago had treated her like his concubine as he would almost rape her when he returned to her from his trips away in the new land that they were living in.

As the days progressed in the garrison, Silvianda's demands for Sir Endevoure to go to the King and plead to him to return her son were getting more over-bearing for our knight until he could not stand it anymore.

It was ten days later, after their return to the garrison, that early one morning Sir Endevoure in full armour had mounted his horse without telling anyone of his ride, that he travelled back to castle Tonest in the hope of retrieving Silvianda's son.

With the garrison gates several miles behind him Sir Endevoure had time to reflect on all those early years of his life when he had lost the most precious people so close to him, that is why he knew how Silvianda felt and he would do everything in his power to help her.

The time soon passed for Sir Endevoure on his ride. Sitting there upon his horse, now out of the forest with a distant view up there on the hill, he was now looking at the Kings colours being flown at half mast from the four turrets of Tonest castle.

"What does this mean?" "I wonder if something as happened to King Hobart?"

With that thought in his mind he spurred his horse again to race down the hill to find out.

As he entered through the castle gates from across the draw bridge, the castle guards suddenly moved quickly to shut these gates behind Sir Endevoure with the result of locking him inside the castle yard.

Just as our Knight was about to draw his sword he noticed several archers pointing their arrows at him from the ramparts, then without warning four guards with long spears moved in close to Sir Endevoure from different directions causing him to be pinned in his saddle by their spear heads against his upper torso.

Then from out of the shadows of the castle walls the familiar voice of Sir Bellingham. "So you thought you could come back here without any recompense of when you were last here did you."

Before Sir Endevoure could reply he was dragged from his horse by several other guards with an almighty clang from his armour as he hit the ground before Sir Bellingham went on to say. "I have orders from the King that if you ever were to show your face again in this castle you were to be taken straight to the cells until the King decides what he will do with you."

Now being lifted as he tried to struggle free the Knight was unable to release himself from their grip as these guards rough handled him towards the castle dungeons.

Just inside the main building where the dungeon's lay, Sir Endevoure was forced down the stone steps of the dungeon where four guards forcefully held him down on the ground while another two stripped his armour off leaving him naked to the elements before throwing him into his cell.

With the cold concrete floor of his cell under him Sir Endevoure was now freezing when he realised that these guards meant business as they were about to move into this small enclosure with their clenched fists.

Watching all this happening while standing back behind the scenes was Sir Bellingham with a cynical smile on his face as he seemed to relish in this Knight's indignation, but the situation was short lived when Ordmin suddenly came down the steps and was horrified to see the Kings cousin was being treated in this way.

Lucky for Ordmin was that he had brought reinforcements with him in the form of Sir Blades and six of his students who were fully armed to the teeth with swords, knives and shields.

These student's could see what was happening so they did not need to be told as they quickly rushed forward pushing these guards to one side before these ruffians had a chance of inflicting severe harm to their fellow Knight Sir Endevoure.

"I would advise you Sir Bellingham to retrieve your dogs or I will not be responsible for my student's actions." Ordmin said as he and Sir Blades stepped forward in front to join his students.

To Sir Bellingham this was an act of treason and he ignored Ordmin's warning as he bellowed to his guards. "Don't just stand there attack these traitor's, kill them where they stand."

As soon as he had gave that order all hell broke out when Ordmin stepped back with Sir Blades into the cell just in time behind his students as Sir Bellingham's guard's rushed forward only to be met with the student's shields being locked together as a steel wall of defiance against their attack.

Now with a stand off from both sides Ordmin with the aid of Sir Blades took the cell's cot's blanket and wrapped it around Sir Endevoure so as to keep his modesty intact before moving him towards his cell door to the outside safety of his student's blockade.

With a lot of difficulty keeping the guards at bay, the student's managed to protect Ordmin with his two Knights after they had scaled the dungeon steps before finally reaching the student's dormitory from the long corridor.

All this time Sir Bellingham was fuming that his authority had been under minded, after all, he was the Kings champion within this castle.

Now with several students guarding the dormitory door from within, Ordmin was finding some clothes for the Knight when he said to Sir Endevoure. "What were you thinking of, coming back here to the castle when you knew the King was upset with you when you took off with Lord Darnley."

Sir Endevoure replied as he started to dress in the clothes that he was given. "I have come back for the boy. His mother is so distraught at losing him, that I have promised her that I will do everything in my power to bring him back. So where is he?"

This was the one question that Ordmin was dreading as he had to come up with a story that would be convincing for this Knight as he reluctantly replied. "I'm sorry but the boy is dead from an accident by no fault of anyone or of the King."

The thought of telling Silvianda that her two year old son had died sent shivers down Sir Endevoure's spine as he asked with tears in his eyes. "How did the boy die?"

"It was a week ago when he was allowed to explore the castle with his minder, only this silly woman averted her eyes for a split second as the boy slipped from the ramparts to the ground below killing him instantly."

Still dubious of this tale Sir Endevoure asked. "Where is this minder now, can I see her?"

"That is a bit awkward the King had her executed for her negligence, so she is no longer with us."

This made life a little uncomfortable for our Knight as he asked. "Is there a chance I could have an audience with the King?"

Suddenly this proposal gave Ordmin an idea of killing two birds with one stone as he replied. "I don't think that would be a good idea, why not let me go and see the King and see if I can get clemency for you if I tell him that you are willing to go back to the garrison on his behalf to tell them that he had no part in Silvianda's son's death and that he as the King had the boy buried to the rear of the castle with his father in the area set aside for royalty."

"That's fine' but how does that help me, how am I going to tell Silvianda that I failed in bringing her son home?"

"You just tell Lord Darnley and his daughter that they are always welcome to come and see the grave of their boy here at the castle once I have found out for sure if the King agrees to all this."

Now beginning to warm up under the clothes given to him earlier, Sir Endevoure thought for a little before saying. "Yes, do it then, but be careful the King does not have you taken prisoner just to spite me for my wrong doings."

As Ordmin with Sir Blades as protection left to see their King, Ordmin thought to himself. "With this story I can get Sir Endevoure free with no one else knowing what really happened to the boy which will help the King out of a predicament and keep him on good terms with the garrison."

Now inside the grand hall after being escorted along the corridor by Sir Bellingham and his guards, Ordmin with Sir Bellingham were now bowing in front of the table of their King who was looking a little cross after being told by Sir Bellingham of Sir Endevoure's return.

"Well Ordmin what have you to say for yourself?" The King said as he picked up a full goblet of wine after his servant had poured it from a large silver jug.

"I beg your highness's forgiveness for today's unfortunate events as I now have a solution for keeping the peace for everybody's future."

The King looking intrigued replied. "Go on then let us see how you get out of this hole you have dug for yourself, well what do you have to say?"

"With your permission I would like it to be for Sir Bellingham and your ears only."

As the King clapped his hands everyone started to leave the grand hall leaving himself, Ordmin and Sir Bellingham there.

After a long discussion with his subordinate the King finally agreed to Ordmin's proposal when he said. "Tell Sir Endevoure if he succeeds in doing this for me he can stay at the garrison to live in peace but only until I call for him on any special quests that I need him to do for me."

"Yes your highness" Ordmin said before bowing again as he left to go through the doors from the hall where he met up again with Sir Blades who had been left outside the hall earlier.

Back at the dormitory of the students Ordmin explained the situation to Sir Endevoure that he was free to go if he obeyed his Kings proposals for the future.

This he was willing to do knowing that it would free him from further repercussions from this demented King.

After Ordmin had sent two of his students to reclaim Sir Endevoure's armour at the dungeons the Black Knight sat down with a good meal amongst the other students before having his armour suited on him for his journey back to the garrison.

Thanking Ordmin for his support and saving him, Sir Endevoure was still not sure if the real truth was told to him, but he knew in his mind that once Silvianda had eventually come to terms with her son's death that life at the garrison would become a lot easier for him to eventually propose marriage to her.

It was late afternoon when Sir Endevoure finally set off on his horse towards the canyon of Vorth to find out if his pet Bisthion was still being fed by the land owner.

After this slight detour to see his Bisthion, who was in the best of health, our Knight spent the night at the land owner's farm house before deciding to set off again the next morning towards the garrison.

Chapter Twenty Four

The Exhumation

Now back to the safety of the garrison Sir Endevoure was not looking forward to telling Silvianda of her son's demise, but he need not have worried because when he stayed the extra night over at Vorth he missed the arrival of Ordmin at the garrison who took it upon himself to give his support to Sir Endevoure's bereavement information.

As our knight entered the manor's main hall he was greeted by a rush towards him of a crying Silvianda who flung her arms around him in despair of just hearing about her son's death.

While Sir Endevoure was comforting her he just realised what was going on as he noticed over her shoulder the sad faces of his friend Ordmin standing there beside Lord Darnley.

"I have just this minute told them of the young boy's death." Ordmin said as he placed his hand upon Lord Darnley's arm.

"I wish you had waited for my return before you gave them the bad news." Sir Endevoure said as he held on to Silvianda to stop her collapsing to the ground in despair.

"I would have, but I thought something had happened to you when you were not here when I arrived." Ordmin replied.

It took most of that day for Sir Endevoure to console Silvianda in her grief until tiredness stepped in when eventually Lord Darnley told Silvianda's maids to put her to bed as he knew that sleep would be a good healer.

Sure enough the next day a change had come over Silvianda as she seemed to have become hardened to the loss of her son when, now awake from her night's sleep, she was demanding Ordmin to tell the King she wanted her son's body to be brought back to the garrison's graveyard.

This demand was going to be a little awkward for Ordmin let alone the King as Ordmin knew that he would have to find an identical body of a boy from somewhere in case Silvianda wanted to see the body when it arrived back at this garrison.

Agreeing to go back Ordmin advised Sir Endevoure for his own safety to stay at the garrison as he was not sure how the King would respond to this demand from Silvianda.

With a full stomach from his morning meal back at the garrison, Ordmin was now riding on his grey horse towards Tonest castle while trying to think of a plan to end any doubts of whether this boy was still alive or not.

By the time he reached the fortress he had the answer he was looking for when he noticed Cretorex the healer outside the castle walls amongst a group of village folk burying a mummified animal.

Dismounting from his horse Ordmin approached Cretorex and asked him what was going on and also if he knew of any premature deaths of a two year old child recently.

Lucky for Ordmin was that Cretorex did as there had been a horrific disaster within the same village from where this rabid pet had come to its sticky end of its life after attacking and killing several children.

With this knowledge and the fact that Cretorex was willing to help, Ordmin went straight to the King to see if he would agree to his plan that he had just devised.

Now standing in front of his King after bowing, Ordmin started to explain his predicament and how he thought he knew of a way round it for the good of everyone's sakes.

His idea was to find the right size child, embalm this child, place it in a casket and send it back to the garrison as Silvianda's child in the hope that she would not look beneath the bindings.

To Ordmin's surprise the King thought this was a great idea when he also suggested that the boy's father was to be sent back as well.

Little did Ordmin know was this King was getting a little tired of some of his subjects going to visit his brother's grave and leaving all manner of well wishes upon it, which seemed to annoy him to think that they thought more of his brother than himself as the King.

A day later after the exhumation of Drago's body being placed in large coffin along with the casket of the mummified child, Ordmin had them loaded on to a horse and cart for transportation.

With an escort of four guards and one driver, Ordmin led the way on his grey horse towards the garrison until they were met half way by Sir Endevoure who immediately wanted to know if Ordmin had any trouble in exhuming the body of the young boy.

Once Ordmin had explained the situation, Sir Endevoure was surprised the king had sent Prince Drago's body as well but that did not stop him from keeping his fingers crossed in the hope it would be enough to help Silvianda get over her grieving.

On entering the garrison, Ordmin noticed the crowds with their heads bowed in respect lining the paths on their way to the manor.

By the time the cart with its escort had got to the manor house the escort had grown in size with most of the population of the garrison following it.

Standing there on the front steps of this manor was Lord Darnley with his daughter Silvianda who rushed forward down the steps to the casket in the hope that her son was still alive.

Lord Darnley immediately raised his voice and said. "Ordmin I think you better lift the lid of the casket just to make sure that this is my grandson?"

This was not what Ordmin was looking forward to when he replied. "Yes sir,

Then looking over to his escort, Ordmin demanded. "I need two of you to give me a hand to lift this lid?"

As Lord Darnley pulled his daughter off the casket, Sir Endevoure joined them for the identity of the young boy just before the two men lifted the lid to disclose the mummified corpse.

"What is this? Why has my grandson had his body embalmed in this way? Is something being hidden from us?" Lord Darnley said as he was shocked at seeing so many bindings.

Ordmin was quick to answer when he said to Lord Darnley. "No sir, If I can have a quiet word with you over here I can explain the situation?"

As Ordmin managed to pull Lord Darnley away out of the ears of other's he explained to him that when the boy fell from the ramparts he unfortunately fell amongst the hoofs of some horses that had just returned with their riders from outside the castle walls.

He went on to explain that because of the boy's severe and unsightly injuries the King thought it best to have him embalmed for the mothers sake so that she would not have to see him looking so disfigured in this way.

"Oh I see! Good idea." Lord Darnley said then went on to say. "So who is this body is in the other coffin? And why have you brought it to the garrison?"

"That would be the boy's father Prince Drago Victinours. Our King told me to bring him here so that he could be buried alongside his son."

Even though Lord Darnley disagreed on Drago's short comings he still felt that any man had the right to a decent burial no matter what he had done, that is why after a long discussion between Sir Endevoure and his daughter they all came to the same conclusion that Prince Drago was to be buried in the same grave yard but in a distant corner away from the young boys grave.

Silvianda's son's funeral was to take place the following day, on hearing this Ordmin decided to stay until it had been completed so that he could be sure that his plan for his King had been fulfilled successfully without any repercussions.

The next day with the funeral well under way as they all stood around the grave, Silvianda broke down again crying on Sir Endevoure's shoulder for the loss of her son as she watched the last piece of earth being placed on his casket.

Unbeknown to others Silvianda still did not believe that the child in the casket was her boy, to her there was something about the whole setup that seemed too obvious to be true.

The only way she could be certain would be if she could see the child's face for herself, with that in mind she would wait until it was convenient to do so when no one was around.

As the day progressed when most of the mourners had departed Ordmin decided to say his goodbyes after reassuring Sir Endevoure that if there was anything underhand against this Knight he would somehow bring word to warn him.

It must have been two nights later when Silvianda with the aid of two of her maids slipped out of the manor with no one else around to exhume her son's body in the hope of proving once and for all that it was him.

With the earth still fresh from the burial, the casket was soon exposed as Silviander, with the help of her maids, jumped down into the large hole.

As soon as her maids had lifted the casket lid Silvianda wasted no time in tearing back the binds on the child's face to expose what she had suspected all along, there facing her was a young girl and not her son.

Straight away this gave Silvianda hope that her son was still alive out there somewhere but she decided for his own safety that she with her maids would keep this nights work a secret until the day when it was safe enough to reveal the truth.

Chapter Twenty Five

𝔇𝔢𝔪𝔦𝔰𝔢 𝔬𝔣 𝔚𝔦𝔱𝔠𝔥𝔢𝔰

Now that Silvianda had come to terms with the destiny of her son being alive or not, life in the garrison had become fairly peaceful for Sir Endevoure in those last two years of courting Lord Darnley's daughter, so much so that this Lord was wondering when Sir Endevoure was ever going to propose marriage to Silvianda.

So being a wise man' Lord Darnley devised a plot to encourage the Knight to pop the question to his daughter by sending some of his warriors out of the garrison to many parts of the realm with invitations for possible suitors to visit the garrison for a tournament of archery.

Lord Darnley's idea was that his daughter would have to kiss every winner within their section of making their way to the final, then once the winner of this final was decided this person would receive a kiss with his trophy from Silvianda along with a night of dining with her in the presence of himself as host.

The only problem was Sir Endevoure was useless at archery so when he heard of Lord Darnley's plans he was not a happy man as he decided to leave the garrison that day on his horse to find someone who could enter this tournament on his behalf.

Lucky for him he remembered Ordmin telling him about a Fletcher called Zerak who was living in a village a mile from the castle, this man was said to be handy with a bow and that on many occasions would come to the aid of his King by supplying his men with weapons.

When Sir Endevoure dressed in riding clothes entered the village on his horse he noticed there was no sign of life around the cottages.

He tied his horse to a post after dismounting, he then walked to the nearest cottage door and when he knocked on the door a medium-size, frail, old woman in her eighties with a humped back appeared.

Her hair was long and grey and hung down to the middle part of her back, her face supported a long crooked nose with several warts attached to its apex making it to look a lot larger under her two small green piercing eyes.

She almost fell over her own threshold in excitement as she started to say with her breathe from her narrow lipped mouth smelling of dead fish. "Yes young man what can I do for you?"

"I'm looking for a man called Zerak the Fletcher; do you know which cottage might I find him in?" Replied Sir Endevoure as the old lady almost toppled on top of him if had not been for his quick reaction of supporting her with his arms.

"Thank you my man; yes I believe he lives that way in a small wooden dwelling with a thatched roof on the outskirts of the village, but you are welcome to come in here first for some refreshment before you go there."

Sir Endevoure was just about to reply when out of the corner of his eye in some bushes nearby he noticed several villagers beckoning to him to come their way.

Fearing that something was amiss with the old lady Sir Endevoure edged backwards as he replied. "That is very kind of you but I cannot stop at this moment as I am on an urgent mission for his majesty the King."

As soon as he had refused her hospitality, this woman suddenly lurched forward with her nails protruding from her fingers along with a mouth full of sharp teeth; only to miss Sir Endevoure as he side stepped out of her way to allow our Knight with this old lady nearly on the ground to quickly draw his sword from its sheath, then with a sudden rush of adrenaline swung this sword down to take the head off this unsightly hag.

The cheer of relief from the villagers in the bushes was short lived from the annihilation of this witch as several more unsightly beings started to appear from other cottages nearby.

With blood still dripping from his sword, Sir Endevoure turned to face his worst nightmare of his life as he was outnumbered seven to one by these monstrous beings charging at him.

Now thinking he had walked into a situation that he was never going to escape from, Sir Endevoure was suddenly relieved when a lone archer from several cottages down started firing arrows into the bodies of these witches with the immediate result that some of the arrows found their way through two of the witches' heads.

This first attack from Sir Endevoure on these devils was what the villagers were waiting for when suddenly from out of their hiding places there appeared a crowd of the villagers with farming tools such as pitch forks, rakes, spades and axes in a ferocious attack on the remaining witches.

Now being attacked from all sides, these old cronies lost three more of their kind before the last remaining two managed to escape from these villagers into a forest nearby.

With their threat diminished, the people of the village cheered as they crowded around Sir Endevoure, lifting him on their shoulders as a celebration of victory.

Now in the air above everybody's heads our Knight was lucky when his own head was missed by inches by a thunderbolt just aimed at him from out of the trees of the nearby forest.

The crowd dispersed quickly from this sudden shock of attack. Sir Endevoure fell from their shoulders to the ground only to witness the carnage of the thunderbolt's destruction of a nearby cottage.

By now the lone archer had arrived to help when he grabbed hold of Sir Endevoure by the arm to raise our Knight from the ground before saying. "Did you see where that came from?"

Before our Knight could answer another bolt fell short of its targets when it hit a fence just to the side of our two heroes.

"That was close!" Said the archer then went on to say. "We better take cover or the next one could be the one that hits us."

"I think you're right, follow me I have a plan." Replied Sir Endevoure as he urged the archer towards the rear of the cottages for a circular assault of the forest where the thunderbolts had come from.

Now out of site in this forest our pair of hunters separated to surprise the last of the witches before these hags had a chance of completely flattening the village.

Looking through the long grass after crawling, both archer and Knight sighted from different positions, one of these witches conjuring up, in her hands, these powerful blasts of destructions.

Using hand signals to the archer to tell him to stay down, Sir Endevoure rose to his feet with sword in his hand before charging towards the witch in an attempt to kill her.

For the time it took for our Knight to reach his target was when the second witch appeared from her hiding place along with her out stretched talons aimed at our Knight's throat.

That is when the archer stood up with his bow before letting go his arrow that flew straight into the second witches stomach, trouble was it did not kill her outright as she managed to pierce a hole into Sir Endevoure's arm just as he was retrieving his sword from the first witch's heart.

As Sir Endevoure winced with pain from this wound the witch's other hand of talons swung round to our Knight's chest in an attempt to push him to the ground but was stopped by the archer sending his second arrow into this same witch's eye which, on contact, this arrow travelled straight through her skull to the other side with the result of pinning her to a tree like a hanging pheasant.

Falling to his knees in pain, Sir Endevoure was suddenly exhausted as the venom from the dead witch's talon had started to enter his bloodstream.

On realising this, the archer, a tall thin dark haired man who had a menacing stare, helped our Knight out of the forest then down to his cottage at the far end of the village where on entering his dwelling was met by his chubby good looking wife with blond hair who at first glance thought Sir Endevoure was drunk until her husband pointed to her this Knights unsightly wound just before Sir Endevoure passed out.

The next thing Sir Endevoure knew was when he was awakened on a rugged ground sheet situated in front of a small fire place with his arm bandaged along with the noise of children running about in the next room.

"Ah you are awake, how do you feel sir?" The archer said as he stood there in front of some of the villagers with his arm around his wife.

"A little sore, where are we?" Replied Sir Endevoure as he was adjusting his eyes to the light.

"You are in my cottage, sorry, let me introduce ourselves, my name is Zerak the Fletcher and this is my wife Leacia who if it was not for her surgical pulses taking the poison out of you, you would be dead by now."

"Then your wife has my gratitude for saving me."

"No sir it is us the whole village that should be thanking you for saving us from those demons. By the way who have we the honour of addressing?"

"They call me Sir Endevoure also known as the Black Knight."

As Sir Endevoure lifted himself up from the floor' Zerak began to explain to him that these witches had appeared a week ago disguised as young maidens that were willing to help any family in need of their services as child minders or cleaners, after several days of helping their households these young maidens changed back into their normal form as witches. The reason they were there in the first place was to start devouring some of the young children with the result of satisfying their lust for young tender flesh.

After the first attack these families were forced out of their homes as the witches were content to stay around for the opportunity of catching any more of these children that happened to come their way.

Now that Sir Endevoure knew the story of why he had been forced to defend his self he then gave the reason for his visit to this village in the hope of contracting the services of this very man in front of him who had just helped him kill the witch's.

Zerak agreed to this challenge, he was only too willing to help this saviour of their village, anyway he was only too glad to get some archery practice in for any future problems that might occur.

Zerak sent his five year old son, called Favour, to fetch our Knights' horse, a blond good looking boy that was small for his age as well as being his youngest child with four sisters. Our archer finally said his goodbyes to his family before stepping out to see his son had just returned with the horse and was in the process of handing over the reins to Sir Endevoure.

Little did our Knight know as he left this village that day was that this blond child would grow up one day to become a famous Knight of integrity, helping others out of their own problems.

Chapter Twenty Six

Archer's Tournament

The darkness of the night was beginning to appear after Zerak had ran beside Sir Endevoure's horse for several miles before both runner and rider appeared out of the forest to the sight of the garrison.

This was not the first time that Zerak had been here, he in his early years was one of the many who helped set up the original perimeters of this fortress.

That is why little did our Knight know was that Zerak was well known to Lord Darnley as one of the finest archer's in these lands.

Inside the manor next morning, after the night before when Sir Endevoure had allowed Zerak to be a guest in his room for sleeping, Sir Endevoure went and introduced his champion to the Lord so that there would be no illusion that he was going to do all he could to win this tournament.

"I don't believe it well look at what has just turned up after all this time, its Zerak my favourite archer, what are you doing here?" Lord Darnley said as Zerak and our Knight approached the large table where the Lord, with his daughter, was having his morning meal.

"Yes my Lord I am a guest of Sir Endevoure who has taken me for his champion in your archery tournament." Replied Zerak as his mouth started to water at the sight of all the succulent meat that Lord Darnley was eating.

Almost choking on this food with a small cough Lord Darnley then turned his attention towards Sir Endevoure. "Is this true? I don't know if that is in the rules."

Before the Lord could finish his sentence Silvianda remarked. "Oh let him compete on Gettard's behalf I am sure there must be other experienced archers coming to this tournament of yours that have just as good a chance as Zerak."

With the Lord agreeing Silvianda invited Zerak to sit down at their table seeing as Sir Endevoure had already sat down for some food.

After the meal Zerak used the rest of this day as practice for his archery to help him in the next day's tournament.

The next day was a sunny day as the gates of the garrison were opened for the outside area of ten distant targets to all contestants as they came from far and wide from many lands just to see if they had the skill of being the best archer.

With the stands positioned against the outside timbered walls Lord Darnley with his guests as spectators sat there watching as the day of archery progressed with many of the contestant's in their heats having faltered in their attempt of winning a kiss from Silvianda.

Problem was that when a kiss was given for a heat win our Knight's face turned red with rage much to the delight of Lord Darnley.

By the time the final of the heats was reached Zerak had already received four kisses from Silvianda and these were not just pecks on the cheek, because knowing that Zerak was Sir Endevoure's champion Silvianda had gone all out for a long lasting kisses on the lips much to Zerak's delight.

Now lined up between five other archers Zerak watched the targets being moved further away by another two yards before taking his turn after the first two archers had already fired with both of them only hitting the outer ring.

As Zerak's first arrow out of three hit the edge side of his bulls eye the marksman to the left of him hit the centre of his bulls' eye which left the last marksmen in this line up only hitting his outer circle.

It seemed that the extra distance was causing problems for most of these marksmen when on their second arrows, Zerak was the only one that managed to hit the centre of his target making it one all in a draw between him and the archer next to him.

That is when Sir Endevoure approached Zerak to give him some encouragement by promising him an extra reward of a horse to take back to the villagers for ploughing their fields.

Three of the archers gave up which left Zerak and this man next to him to take their last arrow, but before they took aim these targets were moved further away by another yard.

As Zerak was to go first he drew his longbow back as far as he was able to knowing that it was almost impossible to hit any target at this distance.

When his arrow finally hit the target it was just shy of the bulls' eye because of that he really thought he had lost until his competitor did the same with his arrow after screwing his eyes up so much at this new distance that it looked as though he was having a job to see his target at all.

As the crowds cheered every time that an arrow hit its target, Zerak and his opponent were told to take another arrow each for a forth go, that is when Zerak had an idea of how to take the advantage over this other archer when he noticed some large flat stones over to one side on the ground, placing his bow over his shoulder then walking away from his starting line Zerak lifted with both hands one of these stones and placed it behind his line then standing on this stone he set his arrow into his bow and fired.

Now that Zerak's arrow was fired from higher level it compensated for the extra distance when it hit its target dead centre of the bulls eye to the sudden surprise of the crowd, they cheered in disbelief at what they were witnessing.

Before his rival was about to fire Zerak said to him. "Why not try the same as I did you'll find it a lot easier to hit the target."

This archer just shrugged his shoulders and ignored Zerak's advice before letting his arrow fly from his bow with the result of his arrow hitting the lower part of his target.

A great cheer from the stands was heard as Zerak made his way towards his prize from Silvianda sitting there with her father in the middle of these stands.

As Zerak received his trophy he also bent forward for his final kiss until Sir Endevoure intervened when he nudged Zerak to one side and said. "You are entitled to this trophy but I think you have had enough kisses for one day."

Zerak started to laugh at this Knight's jealousy as he replied. "Well you kiss her then and why don't you ask her to marry you?"

As soon as this was said Lord Darnley added his comment. "Yes it's about time you proposed, I've been waiting for the day you got off your backside and went for it."

Feeling embarrassed by all the onlookers Sir Endevoure had no option but to propose to Silvianda.

Now kneeling on one knee this Knight held his hand out to take Silvianda's hand before saying the immortal words. "Will you marry me Silvianda dearest?"

With her red face Silvianda replied. "Of course I will, but when?"

"As soon as possible, if your father agrees?"

Lord Darnley raised his arms in the air with joy while shouting out. "In forty days would be a good time, I shall invite everybody, and we shall have the biggest wedding here at the garrison that anyone has ever seen before."

As this happy day progressed when all the stalls had been dismantled after the departure of spectators, Lord Darnley kept his word that evening for the winner of the tournament as Zerak sat at his table alongside Silvianda for his meal.

But because of the special circumstances Zerak agreed that Sir Endevoure should sit on the other side of his betrothed to make sure that there was no more jealousy between either of them anymore.

When the nights celebration was over as everybody retired to their rooms Sir Endevoure told Zerak he wanted him as his guardian at this wedding and he was to bring his family along with him.

Chapter Twenty Seven

The Marriage

Sure enough forty days later when most of the invitations had been accepted, our Lord was not a happy as the King had refused his invitation with his lame excuse for not leaving his castle. The King had sent a message back to our Lord saying that, a Knight such as Sir Endevoure should hold his marriage inside the castle walls and not in some wooden outpost in the middle of nowhere.

Silvianda told her father that he should not be bothered with such a statement from a King who had forcibly taken her son from her on that horrendous day two years ago.

The morning of the wedding was here. Many of the guests stood on either side of a gangway made for them outside, facing the manor, in expectation of the bride and groom to arrive from one of the out houses nearby.

At the same time Lord Darnley was waiting with the holy man on the top of the steps at the front of the manor in readiness for the service of marriage.

With the bellowing sound of two large horns from guards at the opposite corner ends of this manor, Zerak, as guardian, suddenly appeared out from a house nearby only to step to one side to take up his position from behind for Silvianda as she emerged from the same house while holding on tightly to Sir Endevoure's left arm.

This bride to be was as pretty as the day she was born, with her long dark shiny hair supporting a white daisy tiara headdress that seemed to compliment her long light blue flowing silk dress with its daisy train to the rear that was being supported by two maids of honour who were also in blue carrying their bouquets of white daisies.

As for Sir Endevoure, his attire was simple with his head being with no hat to his long blue tunic that was held together in the middle with a large belt for holding his decorated sheath with its knife; under his tunic were light brown britches that had straps to his calves for his long sandaled boots.

Now walking at a slow pace through this gangway of guests the bridal procession was greeted with enormous claps of joy before its bride and groom eventually stood together at the bottom of the steps in front of the holy man in readiness for his blessing.

Standing there on these manor steps in his best clothes, Lord Darnley, with his guards behind him, had tears in his eyes as he gave a little wink to his daughter just before the holy man started with his service as he said at the top of his voice. "Is there anyone here knows of any reason this couple should not be married?"

There was dead silence, especially when Zerak turned around and gave the onlookers that stare of his as a warning.

After a short time of no response from the guests the holy man went on and asked the same question to the bride and groom before saying. "Sir Gettard Endevoure wilt thou have this woman to thy wedded wife, wilt thou love her; honour her, keep her and guard her in health and in sickness as a husband should a wife, and forsaking all others on account of her, keep thee only unto her, so long as ye both shall live?"

"I will." Sir Endevoure replied.

Then looking towards Silvianda this holy man asked her of the same questions for her husband to be in ready for their wedding vows.

Silvianda's reply was the same as her grooms. "I will."

Then the holy man said to Sir Endevoure. "Repeat these words after me; I now take thee to my wedded wife, to have and to hold from this day forward, for better, for poorer, in sickness, and in health, till death us do part, if thee as this holy man will ordain it and thereto I plight thee my troth."

Then moving his attention to Silvianda the holy man said. "Repeat after me; I take thee to my wedded husband, to have and to hold from this day forward, for better, for poorer, in sickness, and in health, till death us do part, if thee as this holy man will ordain it and thereto I plight thee my troth."

Then the holy man turned and asked Lord Darnley. "My Lord do you have the ring?"

As Lord Darnley gave the ring to this holy man, he blessed it before bending down to hand it over the steps to Sir Endevoure who then proceeded to place this ring on the finger of Silvianda.

As soon as this ring had found its finger there were cheers from the crowd just before this holy man went on to say. "I now pronounce thee both man and wife; you may kiss your bride."

After their romantic kiss the guests started to move forward to congratulate the happy couple, at that very moment Silvianda proceeded to lift her long dress at the front where she slipped off a blue garter that was a gift from her now new husband, then with an almighty throw Silvianda sent this garter into the cheering guests which created a bit of a skirmish for a time until someone must have hid this garter from view.

As the maids of honour along with Zerak avoided this rush by running up the manor steps to join Lord Darnley, this joyful crowd then proceeded to lift the married couple on to their shoulders to take them to the chapel at the back of the manor for their blessing from the holy man.

By the time this ceremony had been completed the servants at the manor had just finished preparing the tables for the wedding feast.

That is when on hearing that all the tables were ready for his guests; Lord Darnley decided it was now time to invite everybody into the manor for their long awaited feast for celebrating this wonderful and happy day.

Inside the main hall was the large table situated suitably at the far end facing the entrance doors, this top table was accompanied with eight smaller tables joined together in two rows on each of the side walls of this hall.

With music playing from a small instrumental group of two musicians situated at the side of the entrance the wedding party proceeded to enter with the manor minstrel leading the way as an usher to show all the guests where seats were situated.

Now all in their seats the guests were in full view of the top table were the newlyweds were centred with Lord Darnley alongside the holy man to their right, on the left of Sir Endevoure was Zerak who for him being a commoner was a great honour to be on this table as his wife and children were seated at the end of one of the side tables.

With several taps of his silver tankard on the table for silence in the grand hall, Lord Darnley stood up to instruct his minstrel to make the speech on his behalf.

"Lord, Ladies and Gentlemen Lord Darnley would like to thank you all for coming this day for his daughter's wedding between her as Lady Silvianda and her husband Sir Gettard Endevoure. He would also like you all to know that in all the time that he has known this knight he has been worthy in courage and integrity so as Lord Protector of this garrison he would like to inform you all from this day on that Sir Endevoure will now hold the rank of advisor for his warriors in the face of battles that may befall this garrison. If Sir Endevoure would care to stand for his Lordship he will now present to you Lady Silvianda's dowry."

As Sir Endevoure stood up there was loud cheers with clapping from the guests as Lord Darnley handed over a large cloth bag of gold coins, when on taking this gold Sir Endevoure was surprised from the big hug this Lord gave him along with the words. "You are now my daughter's keeper, be sure to treat her right or you will have me to reckon with."

Managing to pull himself away from this bear hug the Knight replied. "You have my word; anyway that was part of my vows. I do not treat them lightly."

Satisfied by the Knights' answer the Lord then said to his guests. "Right everyone, it's time to eat, get stuck in and enjoy."

The clapping suddenly stopped as the guests started to dive into the food prepared for them which consisted of peacocks, pig meat, beef, cooked fruit and vegetables accompanied with large bowls of boiling hot stews and not forgetting the bread for dipping into all their jugs of wine that were flowing from the large barrels positioned at one corner of the hall.

All the time this party was in progress the manor jester was fooling around the tables pretending to be some sort of hungry animal as most of the guests responded with throwing their left-over's at him.

As day became night the party with its revellers clapped as Sir Endevoure lifted Silvianda into his arms from her seat before setting off to their bed chamber for their romantic evening of love.

It was not long after that the guests decided to stagger from their partying in an effort towards their homes leaving only Lord Darnley laying there with two servant girls as company flat out across some of the empty platters on the large table much to his guards delight when one of them was heard to say. "Never knew the Lord still had it in him."

Chapter Twenty Eight

𝕭𝖞 𝕻𝖊𝖆𝖈𝖊𝖋𝖚𝖑 𝕸𝖊𝖆𝖓𝖘

Over the next few years Sir Endevoure found life difficult as his loyalties between castle and garrison were being tested to the limits of his capabilities when on several occasions the Kings demands would conflict with Lord Darnley's.

It was on one of these tasks that this Knight decided he'd had enough of being an errand boy when he was instructed by his King to assassinate Lord Darnley by dropping some poison into his father in law's wine.

Rather than telling Lord Darnley of the Kings intentions towards him which would certainly have started a war, Sir Endevoure decided to create a situation that would require the services of both King and Lord in a joint venture of having to help each other out of a crisis.

With the help from Zerak and some of his villagers who as it happened were knowledgeable in the lay of the land, these villagers set off early one day with Zerak leading one group and Sir Endevoure leading the other half to find out where the water's origins were which supplied each of these fortresses drinking wells.

Lucky for both groups is that they soon found that both water courses came from the same place far away up in the hills from an underground stream before travelling through the forests until it reached each of the clearings where it eventually flowed to the wells in both garrison and castle.

With this knowledge, Zerak organized his villager's to divert this water course by blocking it with large boulders which sent the water in the opposite direction.

Two days later and now with both settlement's wells depleted of water Sir Endevoure wrote separate anonymous letter's on parchment that were sent immediately by arrows to each of these fortresses stating that if either Lord Darnley or King Hobart did not pay a substantial ransom then a great famine would befall both of their communities.

Now that the bait was set it did not take long before Lord Darnley approached Sir Endevoure with instructions for him to visit the castle and see if Ordmin had any idea of if the King was responsible for the drop in water levels in his water holes and the delivery of this arrowed message.

Problem was that Sir Endevoure was not sure on how the King was going to react towards him when he eventually entered the castle walls as he had not fulfilled his request of his assassination towards Lord Darnley, with this in mind he asked Zerak to allow him to be disguised as an apprentice for one of Zerak's many visits of delivering weapons to this castle.

Dressed as a hooded serf with a long artificial beard, Sir Endevoure still armed with his sword hidden under his long smock was now pushing a large cart full of weapons alongside Zerak while passing through the massive gates at the castle in front of the sinister gaze of two guards standing there looking for intruders to this fortress.

"Hello Zerak who's this with you?" One of the guards said as they had instructions to question any strangers that passed their way.

"He is harmless, he is my new helper called Hoc, It's no good talking to him he is unable to speak due to an illness he had when he was young."

Taking Zerak's word as true both guards allowed them through to make their way to the armoury where both archer and Knight started to empty the cart of weapons with the help from the keeper of arms.

With the cart empty Zerak asked the keeper if he would take them both to the main building for contacting Ordmin as they knew that on their own they had no authorisation of entering that building.

"I am sorry I shall get into trouble if I take you both inside, but don't worry I'll see if I can fetch him here for you."

Sure enough several minutes later the keeper returned with Ordmin, realising that Zerak's serf was Sir Endevoure, Ordmin told this keeper he was no longer needed and that he could have the rest of the day off.

"Right you pair of idiot's what sort of game are you up to?" Ordmin said as he never was a patient man.

Explaining to Ordmin was not easy for Sir Endevoure until his ex master realised that his Knight of Black had been left over the years in awkward situations that is when Ordmin came up with his own plan of helping Sir Endevoure to bring back a friendlier atmosphere between garrison and Castle.

"I'll tell you now." Ordmin said. "The King has already received your arrow of which he has no idea who sent it, he is also upset that his wine is being drunk at a rapid rate to compensate for the lack of water but because of this he has put the castle on full alert in case of an invasion from the garrison or any other force. So I suggest that Zerak should go home to the safety of his family while you Gettard accompany me to visit the King with a story that Lord Darnley would like to meet his highness with the minimum of men at a neutral spot on the plains between both forest's to talk about the unknown enemy in the hope that both King and Lord will patch up their differences. Then if the King is willing for this meet to go ahead, we shall have to try and get back in time to tell his Lordship the same story."

Sir Endevoure stood there thinking a while until he said. "Do you think this King will go for it, and will he let me leave this castle?"

"We can only but try; anyway I shall do my upmost on seeing that you are not incriminated in any way for your past discretions."

With Zerak well on his way home with his empty cart, Ordmin with Sir Endevoure who discarded his false beard found themselves standing in front of the King sitting at his large table with Sir Bellingham looking on from behind.

"Well did you succeed in what I asked of you?" This King said while looking directly at Sir Endevoure.

"No your highness it was not appropriate at the time as!!" This Black Knight was stopped half way through his sentence from the Kings outburst of yelling.

"Not appropriate! Not appropriate who the hell do you think you are telling me it's not appropriate?"

That is when Ordmin decided to speak on Sir Endevoure's behalf. "Your majesty if I may I would like to inform you that Sir Endevoure has come back here with an urgent message from Lord Darnley that would be for your highnesses advantage."

"Well come on then let us hear what this Knight has to say for himself?"

As Sir Endevoure started to explain Ordmin's scheme this King's temper started to calm especially when Ordmin reassured the King that it was in his own interests to keep on friendly terms with the garrison in case one day he would need their forces as a backup against any enemies that thought they could try their luck against his castle.

Now with the King agreeing, Sir Endevoure was allowed to leave and was now riding on a horse, borrowed from Ordmin, towards the garrison in the hope of persuading Lord Darnley to agree to the same plan.

When he arrived at the garrison all was not well inside while riding on through the settlement as he noticed several queues at the water holes where Lord Darnley's men were rationing out the water to the residents from the ever decreasing supply.

On entering the manor Sir Endevoure's wife Silvianda was there to greet him with news that her father Lord Darley had left the garrison early that morning with a few of his men in search of the problem of why the water was so low.

"Do you know exactly where he went?" Sir Endevoure asked his wife.

"Yes he has gone to the hills beyond the forest, he reckons the water comes from there and he was desperate to find out if the King has interfered with the flow."

"I don't think his highness has, I have just come back from the King he is willing to talk with your father about this very problem."

Silvianda was now looking worried as she replied. "You had better go after my father and tell him about the King before he does something silly."

With this information Sir Endevoure kissed his wife, rushed out of the manor, jumped on to his horse then rode off as fast as he could towards the hills beyond the distant forest.

Sometime later from out of the forest at the base of these hills, Sir Endevoure could see, in the distance, Lord Darnley with his group of men riding on their way down towards him.

As Sir Endevoure approached Lord Darnley he noticed the miserable look his father in-law had, this Knight knew then from past experiences he would have to tread lightly when explaining the present situation to him.

"What are you doing here Gettard?" Lord Darnley asked, as like his daughter since their marriage he had always called this Knight by his first name.

"Silvianda told me that you were here. I have news for you from the King."

Before Sir Endevoure could explain, Lord Darnley exploded with rage when he said while nearly falling off his horse. "Don't talk to me about the King, that pretender has gone too far this time, do you know what he has done? He has only stopped our water from getting to us, it is time I taught that King a lesson."

"I do not think that would be a good idea especially as his highness is willing to meet with you about the same problem. If it was him I am sure he would have seen to it that his castle would still have water of which it has not."

As Sir Endevoure went on to explain in more detail to the Lord his temper started to subside before saying. "Ok you go back and tell the King I'll meet him at the willow copse in the grass plain between the two forests in two days time at midday, also tell him to bring only ten of his men with him, I shall do the same, any wrong doings on his part will be met in kind."

Now that Lord Darnley had set the time and place, Sir Endevoure's plan had started to come together, to him it was good news because from then on it would result in him not having his loyalties being divided.

Sure enough after Sir Endevoure had reported back to the King with him agreeing, it was now the day of this alliance to take place when both King and Lord kept to their promises as they came together at the willow from different directions.

After an hour of talking both men realised that neither of them had any part of the sabotage towards each other's fortresses, with this in mind they both amicably decided in future to help each other out in times of crisis.

Chapter Twenty Nine

Saving of a Pet

As the time passed for Sir Endevoure his services to his King were not now needed as much as they were before the alliance was settled peacefully which gave our Knight more time to visit his pet Bisthion at the canyon of Vorth.

It was eight years later since his marriage to Silvianda that he on one of these visits to this canyon was on his horse in full armour while approaching the steep track that took you down there; Sir Endevoure sensed that all was not right when he heard the overloud snorting sounds from his pet.

By the time Sir Endevoure was near the bottom of this track he knew his senses were right because an unknown unseated Knight's horse charged past in front of his horse to make its way up out of the canyon.

Then looking further over to the far side of this large canyon just outside of its three caves he was just in time to see his pet collapsing to the ground in front of a young boy who seemed to have thrown something into its nostrils.

While this was happening Sir Endevoure also observed another boy running out of the caves to help a Knight up from the ground.

Suddenly without warning this fallen Knight lifted a broad sword from the ground and was making his way towards the Bisthion in a threatening way so much so that Sir Endevoure dropped his visor to his helmet then took his lance from his holster and with a kick of his heels rode at a gallop to save his pet from being killed.

By this time the first boy had parried the Knights' broad sword with his own sword to stop him from taking the Bisthion's head off.

By the time Sir Endevoure had reached this scene the Knight was in the process of eliminating the young boy as he had swung his sword full circle in the direction of the boy's head until our Knight, Sir Endevoure, intervened by shoving the point of his black lance against the breast plate of this irate Knight.

It was only then that Sir Endevoure realised that this stupid Knight was Sir Raymond the Yellow Knight who he remembered used to be a little clumsy and had a job staying on his horse when he used to train back at the castle with him as a student.

"Unless you value your life I would advise you to leave this place, this animal belongs to me if any harm befalls my pet the culprit will feel the wrath of my lance, now clear off you idiot otherwise I will forget you are a Knight." The Black Knight said as he pushed his lance further against Sir Raymond which made him step awkwardly backwards on his heels.

Without saying a word Sir Raymond reluctantly backed off from the animal he so willingly wanted to kill, then turning while struggling with the weight of his armour staggered off into the direction of the steep track.

By this time the other boy a tall stocky youngster with black hair ran over to support his friend who was a short blond hair boy that had at this time stood rigid on the spot from the sight of this huge Black Knight.

"Now you two reprobates let's see what you have done to my pet, for both of your sorry sake's I hope he's not dead."

Recovering from his trance the blond hair boy finally found his voice when he said. "The Bisthion is not dead he is only asleep from a powerful sedative that my uncle the medicine man gave me, I have mixed this potion before so I know that it is harmless."

"Would you be talking about Cretorex the healer? Is he still alive? I thought someone would have killed him by now for stepping on too many toes, he always did take chances with the wrong people."

As he said this it was only then that Sir Endevoure caught sight of the shine from the King's crown lying some distance away in the dirt against some stones.

"Yes it is the King's healer called Cretorex; he has taught me a lot about potions and how to administer them safely." This blond hair boy replied as he noticed the Black Knight's glance over his shoulder before rushing over to pick up the crown from the ground; that is when Sir Endevoure edged his horse over to this boy with his lance pointing towards him.

"You can give me back my crown that you have stolen from the cave, and by the way what is wrong with your friend? Why does he keep staring at me like that? Does he know me from somewhere?"

For some reason the taller of the two boys just stood there with a stern threatening look towards Sir Endevoure so much so that it was unnerving to our Knight as he turned to the boy and said. "What is your problem do you know me boy?"

Without hesitation the smaller blond boy of the two suddenly blurted out for his friend. "He is the Kings nephew he has just recently joined us at the castle you might have known his father some years ago when he was alive."

On hearing that this was the Kings nephew sent shivers down Sir Endevoure's spine, his mind started to work overtime as he thought was this true? Was this the son of Silvianda? Has he survived from all those years ago when he was supposed to have been buried at the garrison? And did Ordmin lie about his death?"

Still having a job to take it all in Sir Endevoure then said. "What are your names?"

Still answering for the taller boy the blond boy replied. "His Name is Ixor and my name is Favour the son of Zerak the Fletcher and I vaguely remember you when you came to our village when I was young, also I believe I went to your wedding."

On hearing Favour's answer Sir Endevoure now feeling awkward and decided to let both boys leave.

"I have changed my mind you can take the crown with you, only do not let me see you both down in this canyon again, is that clear?"

"Yes sir." replied Favour and, "Hmph." Was all that Ixor said still with hatred in his eyes.

As our Knight made sure these two young boys had left his canyon he dismounted from his horse to tend to his pet Bisthion.

"Come on old fellow wake up you can't stay here all day."

With no sign of his pet awakening from his comatose state Sir Endevoure gathered as much wood as he could to make a fire to keep his pet warm.

It must have been at least two hours before his Bisthion managed to stand on his four legs, but these two hours helped because this gave our Knight the time to work out in his mind on how he was going to handle the situation of whether to tell Silvianda that her son was still alive or not.

After making a lot of fuss to his pet Bisthion Sir Endevoure decided it was time for departing to make his way back to the garrison, while riding he had time to think of why Ordmin had told the King where the crown was, as it was only himself and Ordmin that knew exactly where he had placed this crown.

On nearing the garrison Sir Endevoure's problem was decided that he would not tell Silvianda of her son's miraculous appearance for the time being as it would only confuse the situation to the point of her wanting to see her son at the castle.

If that was to happen, who knows what this King would do to her once she was inside the fortress, the King might bring it upon himself to have the mother with her son killed so that he could secure his future upon his throne.

Chapter Thirty

𝔅𝔬𝔬𝔨 𝔞𝔫𝔡 𝔖𝔴𝔬𝔯𝔡

Just less than four more years had passed within this garrison for Sir Endevoure, in all that time his marriage to Silvianda was happy and uneventful so much so that this Knight was starting to look for adventure as he was beginning to feel slightly bored from hardly anything to do except the occasional hunt for food to help with stocking the garrison's kitchens.

As for Lord Darnley who was now beginning to age, he was now more content with the indoor life of frolicking with his female servants much to his daughter's distaste as this would irritate her to the point of complaining more to her father than to any irritations from her husband Sir Endevoure.

Then one day a courier from the castle rode in to the garrison with a message for Sir Endevoure from the King which read that our Knight was to return to the castle with this courier for instructions from the King to perform a quest of importance for saving his realm.

Intrigue plus boredom motivated Sir Endevoure to leave the garrison that day in the hope that this quest the King had for him would relieve him from becoming too complacent in his mundane life.

Several hours later after entering the castle, the guards there told Sir Endevoure the King wanted to see him alone immediately as soon as he arrived but also now being in the castle he was not to talk to anyone.

As these guards escorted Sir Endevoure down the long corridor of the main building they avoided the great hall by leading our Knight to the door of the Kings private chambers whereon after knocking twice by these guards at the door his majesty yelled. "Come in."

"Ah you have got here at long last!" King Hobart said while standing by a small table washing his hands in a utensil.

"How may I help you your majesty?" Sir Endevoure said while bowing at the same time.

"I would like you to retrieve something for me the only trouble is no one must know that it was me that sent you especially Ordmin."

"Forgive me for asking Sire but why should no one know?"

With the King drying his hands he looked sternly at this Knight when he replied. "Well I know we have had our differences over the past years but you did originally swear allegiance to me in times of danger which is why I need you to go against your old teacher Ordmin this time."

Knowing his King's deviousness from old, Sir Endevoure wondered what he was scheming this time as he replied to his King. "What has Ordmin done to you then your highness?"

"It has come to my attention from my spies that Ordmin without telling me has sent four of his students to retrieve a special book to help aid him in plotting against me, the trouble is that once he has this book he could be a danger towards the garrison as well."

"Sire where do I go to find this book and what is this book called?"

Picking up a rolled parchment from the back of the table, King Hobart started to unroll it before pointing out exactly in which direction our Knight was to go. "This book is called the book of knowledge, it has been hidden in some catacombs many miles away from the castle, if you take this map with you should find this burial place in no time."

As Sir Endevoure took the parchment this King went on to say. "There is one more problem you must never open this book no matter what occurs only because some of those people who have opened it before have regretted it, otherwise I do not care how you obtain it as long as you bring it back here in one piece is that understood?"

"Yes your highness." Sir Endevoure replied while bowing before leaving the Kings chamber where he met the guards outside to escort him back down the corridor again.

It was walking through this corridor our Knight's brain started to work overtime thinking. "This is not like Ordmin, I have never known him to be anything but loyal to the crown, there is more to this quest than the King is letting on, I shall have to tread carefully and take events as they come or I could finish up making matters worse for myself."

Knowing that these catacombs were some distance from either castle or garrison, Sir Endevoure rode back to the garrison to acquire the services of one of Lord Darnley's servants for travelling with him as his squire as a helper to erect a makeshift camp once they had arrived near these burial chambers.

To be a squire for a Knight is a great honour for those that are chosen so that is why our Knight was not short of volunteers when Lord Darnley finally picked the right man for the job out of the long line up of suitors that were standing there outside the manor that evening as Lord Darnley said to Sir Endevoure.

"There you are Gettard this is the man for you his name is Eroguses, he is the strongest servant I have, you'll find him a little slow but reliable on helping you out of any problems that come your way."

Eroguses was a seven foot giant of a man with broad muscular shoulders along with enlarged biceps and thighs on his legs. His only problem was the unsightliness of his facial features, having a cleft lip under a bald head that was caused by an early illness, when he was a child.

As Sir Endevoure approached Eroguses he realised that this man was slightly taller than himself before saying to this servant. "Can you ride a horse because you will need to keep up with me tomorrow as we need to be moving fast to get to my destination for completing this mission?"

"Doh finks I hove riddon bifur fur Lurd Dernley." Eroguses replied with an unusual dialect that really said. "Yes I think I have ridden before for Lord Darnley."

"Good! I shall see you early in the morning then at the stables."

After this encounter from his now new squire Sir Endevoure retired for the night with Silvianda at their chambers in the manor, where she said to him. "You must be careful of what that King asks of you; there has always been an ulterior motive for his missions that he has given you in the past."

"Do not worry yourself I shall be on my guard against anything that comes my way."

Always when Silvianda was worried for our Knight, he in turn would think of her son out there and still alive, little did he know was that Silvianda already felt that her son had not died that day and was out there somewhere.

Early next morning true to his loyalty for his Lord, Eroguses was now at the stables, having already acquired a horse and sledge for carrying the Knight's marquee and was now also in the progress of saddling Sir Endevoure's horse and packing the food for their long journey.

"Ah! You are here." Sir Endevoure remarked as he entered the stables wearing his armour.

"Yer dir everfink is rady." Which meant? "Yes sir everything is ready."

After Eroguses helped Sir Endevoure on to his horse before mounting his own horse with its tethered sledge attached to it from behind, the two riders set off through the garrison gates to make their way to the catacombs.

It was a long day for our riders after they had ridden through several forests then on to a large grass area before arriving at the edge of a stream at the entrance to a valley.

"This seems a good place to make camp for the night." Sir Endevoure said as he struggled from his mount before checking on his parchment to see that they were on the right course.

It did not take long for Eroguses to set up camp for the night, now eating their meal just outside the marquee, Sir Endevoure told Eroguses that he wanted him to stay at this camp for the next day until he had returned after completing his mission but if he did not return within two days Eroguses was to go back to the garrison without him.

Next day there were no goodbyes for Sir Endevoure because of being up so early and with Eroguses snoring so loud' this enormous sleeping squire never heard our Knight leave his marquee.

With the valley well behind him and now riding in his armour through a forest of tall trees Sir Endevoure rode on until he knew he was getting close to the burial chambers.

After dismounting our Knight had another look at his parchment before realising he was almost there, when out of the corner of his eye he noticed a Knight lying fast asleep under a tree in front of the tunnel that led to the catacombs.

Taking some rope from his saddle bag and his sword from his sheath Sir Endevoure crept up behind the Knight who he recognised as Sir Raymond, he held the blade of his sword against this Yellow Knight's throat while whispering in his ear. "Do not move; and keep quiet or I shall have to slit your throat." "Now put your arms back here on either side of the tree."

As Sir Endevoure was tying this Knight's wrists he noticed a familiar looking student at another tree facing him who was laying there sleeping and was in fact Zerak's son called Favour, not wanting to arouse this blond hair boy until he had finished making sure that Sir Raymond's hands were secure our Knight thought it best to place a rag around this Knights mouth to stop him calling out.

With this Knight tied and now stepping softly towards Favour, Sir Endevoure's armour started to make too much noise that it suddenly made this boy jump to his feet with his sword in his hand after being aroused from his sleep.

Now charging towards our Knight, Favour lifted his sword to the air in ready to strike down on Sir Endevoure's helm only he did not expect our Knight to react so quick when he parried Favour's sword with such force that it sent the young boy backwards to the ground.

Lying there helplessly with his sword now firmly under the foot of Sir Endevoure, Favour was now at the mercy of our Knight's sword being pressed against his chest.

"Stand up boy, go and sit down behind Sir Raymond or you could die here if you want to, it is your choice."

Now with Favour taking the sensible option, Sir Endevoure tied the boys hands together with Sir Raymond's before threading the rope through their arms so as to make sure that they could not move.

Before placing the gag around Favour's mouth Sir Endevoure asked the boy if it was Ordmin that had sent them here to the catacombs.

After a little persuasion from our Knight, Favour decided that Sir Endevoure had been duped by the King into thinking that Ordmin was a traitor, because after the truth had been told that the King had sent everyone after the same book in the hope of killing off Sir Endevoure or his nephew who was at this time in the burial chambers.

Sir Endevoure then decided after placing the gag around Favour's mouth that he should obtain this book for himself in the hope of keeping it safe by placing it in the hands of Lord Darnley.

The quietness of the day was peaceful for Sir Endevoure as he stood one side of the tunnel entrance waiting for Ixor to appear until the smell of rotten eggs hit his nose that was followed with the appearance of this boy who was at the same time shielding his eyes with his hand as he came into the brightness of the daylight.

Before Ixor had a chance to see properly Sir Endevoure grabbed him from behind with his sword at this boy's throat before saying. "If you value your life you'll hand the book over to me."

With this threat to his life Ixor lifted the large book from his belt then handed it over his shoulder to Sir Endevoure' only to receive a hard blow to his head as a thank you from the hilt of the Knight's sword.

With Ixor concussed on the ground Sir Endevoure gave a warning after going back to the tree to Favour and Sir Raymond that if they were to follow him they would certainly rue the day that they did.

Placing this large brown book of knowledge that had no inscription upon its cover into his saddle bag, Sir Endevoure mounted his horse again and rode back to his marquee.

Chapter Thirty One

Home Coming

On nearing his marquee from within the valley Sir Endevoure caught site of black smoke billowing into the midday sky from the direction of his camp which urged him to speed his horse into a gallop before coming into view of his squire screaming whilst being strapped to a steak centred within this roaring fire.

By the time our Knight dismounted his squire, who he had become fond of, had already died from smoke inhalation as his head was now tilted to the ground.

As the blood boiled in our Knight's veins for revenge' Sir Endevoure was in luck, the perpetrators were still in the camp as he knew from all the commotion coming from inside his marquee. Sir Endevoure, with sword in hand, threw back the canopy flap and discovered three scruffy men pilfering amongst his personal belongings.

"You have made the biggest mistake of your lives." Sir Endevoure said as he dispatched the one that was near him with his sword splitting this man's head in half, now seeing their accomplice dead these other two men charged at Sir Endevoure with their weapons consisting of one axe and one dagger.

The axe just missed Sir Endevoure's head as he dodged to one side before thrusting his sword forward into the second mans throat, with blood everywhere the third man thought it better to try and escape this Knight's wrath by trying to dive under the side of the marquee which, of course, was too late because Sir Endevoure stamped his heavy foot onto this man's back while retrieving his sword from the larynx of the second man only to shove the same sword down hard between the third man's shoulder blades, just missing his own foot which was lucky for our Knight as his sword was always kept sharp.

That afternoon was a sad time for our Knight as he cut down the charred body of his squire, Eroguses; now placing him in a grave that he had dug earlier Sir Endevoure then went about cleaning his camp up from all the blood that was spilt in his marquee, lucky for him was the stream nearby as the amount of blood needed plenty of water.

After the disposal of three bodies in a shallow grave well away from his camp, Sir Endevoure was now tired from all this work of lifting, it was then he remembered about the book that he had obtained earlier from Ixor.

Taking this book from his saddle bag before sitting in his marquee, our Knight furtively opened this book to a blinding light which immediately took him to a place of uncomfortable presence of inner being for his future life.

By the time Sir Endevoure awoke from this trance it was the next morning after he had seen his whole life unfold in front of him, the knowing of which he would never be able to tell to those who were closest to him for fear that it would endanger their lives.

With the morning chorus of wild life outside his shelter along with the smell of dew drawing the scent from flowering plants, our Knight started to feel at peace within himself for the first time until that harmony was rudely awakened with the sudden sound of a clang on his shield that was placed strategically outside his marquee.

"Who the devil is that?" He said out loud forgetting there was no one listening, or so he thought until a voice was heard from outside.

"Come out and fight you murdering coward, this day will be your last."

Picking up his helmet Sir Endevoure stepped out of his marquee to the sight of the young boy Ixor sitting astride a horse that he had borrowed from Sir Raymond.

"Go away boy you are not man enough to take me on, go back to your nursery before you do something that you'll regret." Our Knight said as he placed his helm on his head along with lifting his shield from the ground.

Ixor's face went red with rage as he replied while jumping from his horse with sword and shield. "It was you who killed my parents, now prepare to die you dog."

Then Ixor with a thrust with his sword to Sir Endevoure's body was unable to make contact because our knight covered the blow with his shield before charging towards this boy with this same shield as a battering ram, now with the full force of his weight behind this shield our Knight sent Ixor backwards to the ground before sitting across Ixor's body with the shield again on its edge at the boys throat.

With his arms pinned under the weight of the Knight, Ixor was unable to move as Sir Endevoure started to explain the circumstances about his early years. "I think you will find it was not my idea to kill your parents but that of the King who has been lying to you all this time, I was a pawn like most of us for this Kings bidding to obey him at all times. I still regret to this day the day I killed your father that is why I did not kill you because it was obvious to me that the King wanted you dead as well by sending you on this foolhardy quest." "Now if I let you up and explain to you the real truth about your mother and father will you promise not to keep trying to kill me?"

Now starting to cool down Ixor gave a nod before replying. "Only if you stop treating me like a child"

Cautiously Sir Endevoure released his shield away from Ixor's neck before rising to his feet allowing this young boy to be free of his weight.

The marquee was the place they sat that day for these two adversaries as they began making their peace when our Knight started to explain to Ixor the real truth of what happened all those years ago.

Even after explaining to the boy, Sir Endevoure still had not told him of his mother's existence until he decided to stand up feeling uncomfortable with what he was about to say. "I have something else to tell you, you probably will not like it but I need you to know that your mother is still alive. She became my wife two years after your father died, which is another reason why I could not harm you because you are my stepson and your mother still thinks you were killed all those years ago.

Ixor's sat there stunned for a while in disbelief until he said. "Why did you keep this secret from me when we first met, why tell me now, what am I supposed to do about it?"

"I know you are angry, but I would like to take you to see your mother, that is if you will let me take you. If you do, you could meet your grandfather who, if you would like to know, is Lord Darnley, the Lord in charge of the garrison. It was him who allowed me to be part of his family; you'll find him a strict man but kind hearted too, especially to the population of his garrison."

"So what do you say, will you come?"

Even now Ixor was not sure what to do until curiosity got the better of him when he replied. "I suppose so, how far is it to the garrison and do you think my mother will accept me as her lost son?"

"I'm not sure we'll have to take it as it comes but from now on if you like you can call me dad."

"I'll just call you sir for now if you don't mind." Ixor replied as he was now anxious as to how he was going to be accepted at the garrison.

For the rest of that morning stepfather and son sat there talking about their past experiences along with what the future might bring.

It was in the afternoon they left this marquee standing for another day as they mounted their horses and rode off towards the garrison.

Several hours later, with the evening approaching, our two riders had eventually arrived at the hill overlooking the garrison where Sir Endevoure pointed to the manor. "That is where your mother lives with your grandfather; we should be there before dark."

Sure enough by the time they had ridden through the crowded streets of waving bystanders, Sir Endevoure with Ixor arrived at the steps of the manor, as they dismounted two servants took their reigns and led their horses to the stables just before Lady Silvianda appeared at the top of the manor steps in anticipation of her husband's return.

"I have brought someone to see you." Sir Endevoure said as he, with Ixor, climbed the steps before giving his wife a hug and then a kiss.

"Who is this then?" Lady Silvianda replied as she thought this boy looked familiar.

"This is your son you lost all those years ago, his name is Ixor."

As both mother and son's eyes met the resemblance was apparent to her ladyship as she suddenly pulled Ixor into her arms. "My son, you have come home to me." she cried.

The emotion was too much for Ixor as a small tear dropped from his eye while exchanging this warm embrace with his mother.

That evening Ixor met his grandfather for the first time, while eating their evening meal, before being led on a tour of the manor and its grounds.

It was on this tour that Ixor was shown his father's grave where he stood silently still in front of its dragon topped head stone that read.

"HERE LIES DRAGO VICTINOURS KNIGHT OF THE DRAGON RED."

The emotion of seeing this was too much for Ixor as he tried to cover his sadness when he asked Sir Endevoure. "What did you do with the book of knowledge, have you still got it?"

"No I gave it to your grandfather I believe he has hidden it for good as he said it was too dangerous to be around, anyway I did have a look in it back at the marquee and I was given a vision of you for your future as being our next King, which you should be, as this King, we have now, stole the throne from his older brother who was your father."

"How can I be King now' I cannot go back to the castle without that book, he will have me killed?"

"He wanted you dead anyway that is why I have brought you here to train you myself in warfare so that one day you will be able to reclaim your throne."

"What if I don't want to be King?"

"Don't be silly you are the rightful heir to the throne; anyway the whole garrison is behind you with their support, so you can start your training tomorrow."

Ixor was now more confident that he knew the garrison was behind him when he said. "Now that I know this garrison is for me I shall stay here then."

"Good that's settled." Sir Endevoure replied while giving a sigh of relief.

Chapter Thirty Two

Rescue of a Princess

There were no reprisals from the King for losing the book of Knowledge in those last two years at the garrison while Sir Endevoure had been teaching Ixor his battle skills, because it was thought that the young boy Favour when he returned to the castle must have told his King that Ixor was killed with the other two students that were sent by him, especially when Sir Raymond returned with no horse after lending it to Ixor.

But it was after those two years on no particular day that Ixor while training in the garrison noticed his long lost friend Favour now armoured up as a Knight and was at this very moment being escorted by two guards towards the manor house.

"Favour what are you doing here?" Ixor shouted as he ran towards his friend.

"Don't worry about me it's you that I am surprised to see, I thought you had been killed when you did not come back that day, the day when you left on Sir Raymond's horse." Sir Favour said before they started reminiscing about old times.

It was then that Sir Endevoure shouted out from where his stepson was previously training. "Ixor come back here you have not finished your daily workout yet."

Sir Favour was shocked to see that Sir Endevoure was here training with his friend as he remarked to Ixor. "I thought you hated that man, why are you with him now?" "It's a long story I can't stop now, I'll tell you after my training session" Ixor replied as he started to run back to our impatient Knight.

Sometime later that night at the table while eating their evening meal all was explained by Lord Darnley as to why Sir Favour had told him that he had been sent by the King to ask for this Lord's help by using Sir Endevoure to rescue a young Princess called Collesta.

Apparently this Princess was on her way with her dowry to marry our King in the hope of an alliance between her father who is a King Plestoe from a faraway land across the seas, until when travelling to the castle she was abducted by ruffians in a forest near to the garrison and now these kidnapper's are asking for a ransom to be paid for her release.

Early the next morning, Sir Endevoure, Ixor, Sir Favour and six of the garrison's warriors set off on their horses to ride towards the forest in the hope of rescuing this Princess Collesta.

Two hours later this band of men were now following a track through this forest until they noticed many carrion flying some distance in front of them, that's when Sir Endevoure told his group to wait while he scouted ahead to see why the birds were flying there.

Further along this track after rounding a bend our Knight came upon the sight of carnage, in front of him about twenty men laid butchered, most of them with arrows protruding from their bodies, the smell was rank from their corpses making them attractive to the carrion above.

Just as our Knight was about to return to his men, a terrifying scream bellowed out from over a small hill as though someone was being tortured which made Sir Endevoure dismount before crawling to the top of this hill. Peering down out of sight he watched in horror the sight of a man being slowly skinned alive by two barbarians in front of thirty onlookers who were laughing and joking. Sickened at the sight of this, our Knight crept on through the undergrowth around these murderous barbarians to a small makeshift hut that he had noticed was there, then parting some branches to the side if this hut he discovered inside a beautiful young girl laying there frightened with her hands and feet tied, her hair was long and black, her features small like a pixie with lips as red as a rose which complimented her beautifully shaped body.

"Hush! Do not make a sound." Sir Endevoure said quietly as he began to cut her bonds with a knife.

Now released from this rope our Knight guided this girl out under the hut only to be met by two scruffy looking ruffians standing there when one of them said. "You are a big fellow, thought you would get away with our bit on the side did you?"

As the Princess collapsed to the ground in despair our Knight drew his sword and then with a swipe took the head off one of these men before bringing this same blade around to sever the other rogues arm, with blood oozing everywhere Sir Endevoure finished the second man off with a thrust through to his stomach.

Trouble was that the noise from this fight had not gone unnoticed when the other barbarians started to run towards our Knight who was beginning to think that this was the end until a sudden shout from Ixor was heard while charging down the hill with his men from all directions. "Attack and kill the swine."

It did not matter that they were outnumbered by five to one because their fury along with their surprise attack was enough to kill more than half of these barbarians before the rest of these ruffians disappeared into thick underbrush with their lives.

As Ixor approached his father in law he said. "It's a good job we got here when we did or it could have been you being skinned alive."

It was then that Ixor noticed how attractive Princess Collesta was to him as he asked her if she was hurt in any way.

Before the Princess could reply Sir Endevoure told Ixor she was not injured and that he should go and cut the skinned man down from the tree and then to help his men bury all the bodies from this camp before going back to bury the dead of the Princess's original escort.

When all the corpses were laid to rest this Princess explained that when she was captured with her manservant some of these barbarians took the coach with its dowry away somewhere and now she was worried that she had let her father down because without these riches the King would no longer want to marry her.

It was then decided by Sir Endevoure to pursue the coach with Ixor along with two warriors while Sir Favour was to return to the garrison with the rest of the men as escort for the Princess.

For some reason Ixor had fallen in love and was reluctant to leave the Princess until Sir Endevoure insisted he required his help for this next task of securing her dowry.

Some distance away after riding through the forest, our Knight and his group, were suddenly showered with a volley of arrows causing them to jump from their mounts but not before one of the two warriors was pierced through the neck by one of these shafts.

Now with one man dead before taking cover behind the trees Sir Endevoure told Ixor. "While I give them something to shoot at I want you to take your man into the under growth and sneak up to them from behind."

Then just as he said this our Knight jumped to his feet and started running from tree to tree, now with arrows trained on Sir Endevoure; Ixor and his partner soon made light work of killing the archers, after creeping out of the bush from behind and slitting their throats.

Now making sure all was clear Ixor called out to his stepfather. "Over here I can see the coach with its horses is in a clearing on other side of this hill."

When all three rescuers reached the coach after walking cautiously towards it, they opened its door where they found the dowry intact consisting of two chests full of gold coins and jewels.

"Now that's what I call a dowry, the Princess's father must be very rich to offer all that wealth, no wonder our King Hobart is keen to marry her. Sir Endevoure remarked before Ixor replied.

"Yes the alliance would make him very powerful to have another realm to protect him."

Just as they started to relax a twig snapped the other side of the coach, where they noticed a barbarian running from his hiding place. Sir Endevoure took his sword from its sheath, throwing this blade into the centre of this man's back, killing him outright.

"Well I hope that is the last of them." Sir Endevoure said as he walked over to retrieve his bloodied sword.

After the burials of their enemy this group of warriors placed their dead comrade in the coach for their journey back to the garrison.

Chapter Thirty Three

$\mathfrak{S}$talemate

The cheers from the population of the garrison was a welcomed sight for our three hero's when they returned that very next morning as they made their way through the streets towards the manor, even though these people meant well our battle hardened conquerors were too tired to really care.

After pulling up with the coach outside the manor, Lady Silvianda standing there with her father hugged her husband on his safe return, whereas Ixor was glad to see Princess Collesta after she had kissed all three men on the cheek for saving her precious dowry.

Later that day Lord Darnley made sure that his dead warrior in the coach was laid to rest in a grave fit for a hero with full garrison honours.

It was obvious to Sir Endevoure that this Princess and Ixor had fallen in love that day after spending most of the time together in each other's company, this, he thought, was going to cause problems, which he found out later to be true as Lord Darnley was persuaded by Ixor to let Princess Collesta stay for a week longer before the Lord's escort had to eventually deliver her to the King in his castle.

By the time the week was up Ixor did not like the idea of releasing this Princess to the King because now she had been told that this King was a lot older than herself she was now in the same mind as her new found love.

Regrettably Ixor was persuaded to let her go after talking it through with Sir Endevoure and Sir Favour. It was decided that Ixor was to wait for four days after these two Knights had delivered this Princess to the King, in that time Sir Endevoure was to ask the King if he would release his hold on this Princess, if there was no news in those four days Ixor would go to the castle himself as a last resort in the hope that this King might change his mind.

When the coach and its party eventually arrived at the castle, Sir Endevoure was approached by several Knights who were training outside the castle walls. One of these Knights was Sir Bellingham, who decided, with his fellow Knights, to escort this coach through the castle gates.

Inside the walls Ordmin was there with the maids to take the Princess to her quarters while at the same time Sir Endevoure along with Sir Favour were escorted by Sir Bellingham straight to the King.

Entering the main hall Sir Endevoure noticed the King was there, sitting behind, at the head of his large table with more armed guards than he usually had.

The King, looking confident with the amount of protection around him, gave a quick nod of his head to some of his guards standing near to Sir Endevoure.

Suddenly these guards pushed past Sir Favour only to surround Sir Endevoure with their swords raised at him as a defence for Sir Bellingham to remove our Knight's sword from its scabbard.

Sir Favour tried to intervene but was told by Sir Bellingham to leave the hall until the King was ready to see him again.

Now with Sir Favour gone the King said to Sir Endevoure. "You thought you could deceive me by not killing the boy and keeping that book, well you were wrong these treasonable acts have a way of reaching my ears, for not carrying out my orders you shall be imprisoned until I decide what to do with you."

As Sir Endevoure was being held by the arms of two guards he could not move when he replied. "But I saved the Princess and brought the dowry here for you surely that would show I am not a traitor."

With smile on his face the King said. "Ahh that was a ruse and you fell for it, did you not realise apart from wanting to marry this Princess who would create an alliance with her father King Plestoe that I also took it as an opportunity to employ the services of those rogues to kidnap her on her way here. That is why I sent Sir Favour to you to help rescue her knowing that you would eventually return here, and here you are."

Then pointing to the hall's doors this King said to his guards. "Take him to the dungeons."

This command was all these guards needed as they dragged the struggling Sir Endevoure off to the dungeons.

It was then that the King told Sir Bellingham to bring back Sir Favour. When Sir Favour returned to the great hall the Knight wanted to know why Sir Endevoure was arrested but was promptly told by the King to mind his own business unless he knew what was good for him as this King insisted he was to go back to the garrison with a message for Ixor that he would only release Sir Endevoure or the Princess if Ixor was to give himself up to him.

While Sir Favour was on his way back to the garrison, Sir Endevoure was stripped of his armour then systematically roughed up in his cell by the guards under Sir Bellingham's supervision.

With two men holding him on either side by his arms, there was a third man punching our Knight in his face and stomach with so much force that Sir Endevoure was soon oblivious of his surroundings.

The last thing he knew was Sir Bellingham saying. "You have had this coming to you for a long time, you are lucky that I don't have you killed if it was not for the King needing you for bargaining with."

As our Knight lay there little did he know that back at the garrison, Ixor on hearing from Favour about the Kings deceit had gathered an army of three hundred men and were now well on their way back towards this castle.

It must have been a lifetime for Sir Endevoure before Ordmin appeared at his cell with news that the King was releasing him to stop the invasion of Ixor's forces now that this young warrior was at his castle walls.

"Can you stand Gettard?" Ordmin asked as he entered this cell with his hand out for support.

"Of course I can, you don't think a beating would keep me down did you. It just gives me more ammunition to defeat this King and his followers. Anyhow why are you here? Or have you just come here to gloat?"

"Certainly not I know we have both gone our separate ways but we both have the same aims as each other which are to put the rightful heir on to the throne. Anyway the King has promised your safe release after I suggested to him to hold a tournament outside the castle walls between yourself and the other Knights in a bid to settle this problem of ownership to this throne."

"You don't think he will keep his promise do you, he's likely to double cross everyone for his own gains." Sir Endevoure said while pushing away Ordmin's hand.

"It's a start let's take it one step at a time we'll just have to be on our guard. Now come on let us get you back to Ixor and tell him about the tournament before the King changes his mind."

Now back in armour again before mounting his horse outside in the castle yard, Sir Endevoure asked Ordmin. "What has the King done with the Princess? Is she safe and can I see her before I go?"

Struggling to mount his own horse with the aid of a squire Ordmin replied. "She is in safe hands with her maids who are on strict instructions from me to stay with her at all times, but I don't think it

245

would be a good idea to see her just yet as it would complicate matters until we have sorted the winner of this tournament."

As the drawbridge was lowered to allow Sir Endevoure and Ordmin out, our Knight suddenly realised the full extent of the seriousness of the situation as he was confronted with the might of Ixor's forces surrounding this castle.

While riding towards Ixor standing there at his marquee our Knight glanced over his shoulder at the sight of the Kings archers looking out from the ramparts at the ready for any onslaught that Ixor's warriors had for them.

"It is good to see you both again but where is Princess Collesta?" Ixor asked as he grabbed the reigns of Ordmin's horse.

"She is at the moment safe with her maids in her chambers; the King has said no harm will come to her as long as you withhold your forces." Ordmin replied while sliding of his horse awkwardly with his legs nearly giving way before carrying on with his message.

"The King has also instructed me to tell you he is willing to give you a compromise that could settle this dispute once and for all."

"Come inside the marquee I'm curious as to what he has to say.

Hello! What has happened to you?" Ixor said after seeing Sir Endevoure's battered face.

"Do not worry about me I shall pay back these bruises in kind once Ordmin has told you what the King has to offer you." Our Knight replied while lowering his head to enter the marquee.

Once inside Ordmin explained how his King had agreed that instead of killing a lot of men on this day it would be far better to hold a tournament for duelling, then the leader of the winning side of this event would lay claim to the throne.

Even though Ixor knew he was short on skilled Knights he agreed to the King's terms.

As Ordmin finished explaining about the organization of this tournament, Sir Endevoure was relishing the thought of meeting Sir Bellingham in combat again as a way of revenge for beating him up.

Chapter Thirty Four

𝕶night against 𝕶night

The next day Ordmin started to organize the construction of the stands for the tournament along the outside walls of the castle.

The decision was made that each side's marquees would be positioned at each end of the joisting lanes.

By that afternoon all was ready as all the competing Knights along with their personal squire's positioned themselves in their marquee areas.

On the side of the King you had Sir Bellingham, Sir Raymond, Sir Blades and five minor Knights, whereas on the opposing side you had Ixor, Sir Endevoure and six of the best horsemen that Ixor could find.

That afternoon the drawbridge was lowered again to allow the King and his personal bodyguards to make their way to their seats in the stands that were centred directly to the side of the four duelling lanes.

The first two duels were decided by lot early that day between two of Ixor's horsemen battling against Sir Blades alongside his partner Sir Bellingham, because of the experience of these two Knights the outcome was inevitable, as both of Ixor's horsemen fell from their horses after receiving blows to their chest plates from their opponents well directed lances much to the delight of the King as he and his followers gave out an enormous cheer while standing up from their seats.

This sign of delight from his majesty was short lived as Sir Endevoure alongside Ixor rode up in line for their duel against two minor Knights whereon, after their duels, there was exactly the same result as the first battle only this time in reverse order as both of the Kings men hit the dirt after flying from their horses.

The third duels were two minor Knights against two of Ixor's horsemen that ended in a draw as both sides lost one man each in this bout.

It was now Sir Raymond's turn sitting on his horse alongside one of his sides minor Knight's in readiness against two more horsemen from the garrison, once again a bad result as both of Ixor's men left their saddles from blows their shields failed to stop.

The King was now getting very excited with the thought of winning as he was now on his feet cheering his head off.

Seeing this Ixor turned to his men telling them that whatever the outcome on this day you are and always will be my champions.

"Do your best just try to stay in one piece?" He said as he watched Sir Endevoure with the last horseman mount up ready for their joust against the opposing end made up of Sir Blades alongside his minor

Knight before they eventually charged towards each other with lances poised for the strike.

This was the first time in this Tournament that two veteran Knight's were competing for supremacy as the Black Knight's lance made contact with the Green Knight's helm knocking him backwards out of his saddle to the ground.

While in the other duelling lane Ixor's horseman had a similar victory over his opponent which left the King looking not as pleased as he was previously because the odds were now even.

Two squires were rushed just in time to carry Sir Blade's off on a stretcher from his comatose state from when he hit the ground before Ixor and Sir Endevoure lined up again for their penultimate duels against Sir Raymond and the last of the minor Knights.

The two sides charged towards each other at such speed that the lances of both Ixor and Sir Raymond just brushed each other's shield with no effect whereas Sir Endevoure again dismounted this new opponent from his experienced thrust of his lance.

Now turning for their second run both Ixor and Sir Raymond charged again with this time Ixor succeeding in powering his lance through shield and rider causing his opponents horse to buckle on its front hoofs which sent the Yellow Knight into a summersault from his horse before landing on to his back into the ground.

Now with only Sir Bellingham left, Ixor decided to let Sir Endevoure have his revenge with the last joust knowing that our Knight's grievance was greater than his own as Ixor confidently remarked. "Anyway if you lose I'll get my chance to have a go, whatever the outcome I'm sure one of us will topple him."

"Don't you worry I'll make sure he tastes the dirt before this days over, It's something I have been looking forward to, his days are numbered you can be sure of it." Sir Endevoure replied as he prepared to ride towards his jousting lane.

It was then that Ixor happened to glance over to see the King giving a signal towards the castle ramparts.

"Now what is he up to I don't think he's going to obey by the rules we'll have to be on our guard for anything underhand."

Ixor thought as he looked back to see both Black and Blue Knight thunder towards each other before their lances both snapped from their direct strikes upon each other's shield.

Riding back to collect another lance both Knights charged again, this time on contact only their horses were left standing after both riders had simultaneously succeeded in knocking each other from their mounts to the ground.

Now with swords drawn these two Knights started to battle on for more than ten minutes until the strength of Sir Endevoure conquered through as he shoved Sir Bellingham to the ground while knocking the Knights helmet off before bringing his sword in line with Sir Bellingham's throat.

Now with the upper hand after Sir Bellingham conceded defeat, Sir Endevoure took the opportunity to say. "Do you swear allegiance to Ixor the true King or would you prefer to die here and now in front of all to see?"

Gasping for air Sir Bellingham still trapped to the ground replied. "I would prefer to live so I better swear allegiance to the new King."

Just as Sir Endevoure helped his opponent to his feet from the cheers of Ixor's warriors these cheers were soon changed into shouts of horror as they all noticed the sight of two henchmen of the Kings guard were holding on either arm of the struggling hysterical Princess from on top of one of the turrets above the ramparts in readiness for the Kings command to throw her to her death.

This action of the King put Ixor's army of warrior's on full alert as they decided to rush forward to protect their mentors with their shields along with their weapons aimed in the direction of the castle.

At the same time King Hobart's bodyguard surrounded him from any harm, Ordmin who was sitting next to his King was pushed to one side out of the way, before turning to his King. "Sire I made a promise on your behalf that the Princess would not be harmed in any way, why have you gone against your promise?"

"Stop whining you old fool, its time I got rid of you." The King said as he nodded to one of his men to thrust his sword into Ordmin's side, which killed the old adviser immediately where he stood.

Now with Ordmin dead on the ground this King averted his attention to the turret over the ramparts as he indicated with a slight gesture of the hand for the men holding Princess Collesta to push her to a certain death.

It was at that very moment that a large bird flew towards this turret carrying Sir Favour on its back; with a loud shrill from its beak this bird swooped down just in time to grab, with its talons, the Princess around her waist before she hit the ground and then with its wings flapping again carried her off towards the trees at the rear of Ixor's forces.

These Knights had always respected Ordmin, killing him in this way the King had gone too far as the opposing Knights now swore allegiance to Ixor their true King, on seeing this change of heart from his Knights, King Hobart surrounded by his bodyguards started to retreat back to the safety of his castle.

At the same time Ixor told his archers to fire a volley of arrows towards this treacherous King before he reached the castle gates. Some of these arrows met their targets with devastating effect as most of his bodyguard received an arrow, now with more than half of his protection dead or wounded an arrow somehow managed to find its way through the barrier of men with the result of striking the King in his arm.

With the drawbridge lowered and now holding his wound the King with the rest of his men limped through the gates to the safety of his castle just in time as the next volley of arrows hit the drawbridge as it was being raised.

Archers from the ramparts retaliated with arrows flying everywhere forcing Ixor's forces to retreat to a safe distance where they regrouped to take up safe positions around the whole perimeter of this castle.

Now fully camped in their marquees to the rear of his men, Ixor discussed his strategies with his Knights for their next move of putting this fortress under siege.

It was decided that Sir Endevoure was to be left in charge while Ixor along with the now recovered Sir Blades were to go searching through the dense forest for the Princess and Sir Favour.

Chapter Thirty Five

Castle under Siege

While Ixor was away Sir Endevoure with the idea from Sir Bellingham had come up with an ingenious plan for scaling the castle walls, the idea was to attack this castle without losing too many men so after chopping down vast numbers of trees for making two large assault towers, large intense fires were lit from the debris of wood chippings that these shelters had made.

Once these fires were well established the stables farriers were told to forge four enormous iron hook eyes for driving into the sides of the castle walls also extra craftsmen were told to weave large quantities of rope from bark fibre and creepers left over from these fallen trees.

It was on the second day of construction that Ixor returned with Sir Blades to the sight of all this activity when on arriving at Sir Endevoure's marquee asked for a meeting to be held with the other Knights to be present.

Now ready to sit down with food and drink being served from their squire's, Sir Endevoure asked Ixor. "Did you find the Princess and is she well?"

"Yes she is well I have sent her back to the garrison with Sir Favour, anyway it looks as though you have been busy while I have been away. Whose idea was it to build those towers and what are those iron rings for?"

"Ah you will see tomorrow its one of Sir Bellingham's brain child idea's, he has been quite helpful while you have been away."

Sir Endevoure replied as he sat down next to Ixor before telling a squire to serve up the food and wine.

Next day Ixor's archers were strategically positioned in front of the castle behind their shields while unleashing a barrage of arrows at the ramparts to keep the heads down of the castle's inhabitants.

Then under the protection of these arrows two groups of eight men carrying the four iron rings rushed forward to each of the two turrets positioned at either end of the castle, now under the safety of the base of these walls they started to ram in two on each tower of these irons with large anvil hammers.

Stones, rocks and other dangerous items were being thrown from the turrets but to no avail because the invaders were too close to the base of the walls making it impossible to reach them.

With all the rings firmly in place Ixor's men managed to safely escape back to behind the archer's shields where they were greeted with cheers from their own forces.

Satisfied his men had succeeded Sir Endevoure turned to Ixor and the other Knights and said. "Tonight in the dark I shall send some more men with those four long ropes to thread through these rings in ready for the sides of our nearly finished towers."

After the success of that night when the ropes were in place, Sir Bellingham informed the other Knights that the invasion towers would be ready in three days time before saying to Sir Endevoure. "Let us hope the weather turns to rain it would be to our advantage as we do not need the enemy to use fire arrows against us when we pull these towers into position."

"Good idea it's decided then we wait for rain then on that day we attack in force, make sure everyone stays on high alert for the next few days in case the enemy decides to come out of their castle with surprise attack." Sir Endevoure said as he bent over to feel the strength of these thick ropes.

More than a week passed and in that time the drawbridge was lowered twice for its castle riders to make a sudden attack against Ixor's forces but were driven back by the supremacy of their opposition's might of defence.

At last the day came when the heavens opened as the rain dropped like a waterfall it was then that Ixor instructed his Knights to tell the men to be ready with their invasion towers.

With the ropes threaded from the sides of these manned towers down to the iron rings at the castle then back again, these rope ends were then tethered to four groups of six heavy set horses, now being under the lash these horses began to pull in the opposite direction of this castle before this wet weather made it too muddy for pulling these heavily armed towers.

As these towers edged closer to both turrets the castle archers found it difficult to fire upwards against the driving rain to a structure that was taller than their own turret, but for Ixor's archers it was a blessing as now they had the advantage of shooting their arrows downward towards the ramparts.

After killing or wounding many of the Kings men in this cross fire of arrows, a large ramp was lowered simultaneously from just under the top level of both of these towers to allow Ixor's infantrymen to jump across to these ramparts to strike with their weapons against the Kings demoralised army.

Working their way through the ramparts this attack was bloody and decisive as many of the Kings' men were too weak from lack of food due to their imprisonment by this siege of their castle.

With the ramparts taken the castle drawbridge was soon lowered for a quick defeat as the rest of the castle inhabitants surrendered under a white flag just before the gates were opened to Ixor's cavalry of Knights when they charged through these castle grounds carrying their lances.

As Ixor rode in with Sir Endevoure it was obvious to him that the residents of the castle were starving they looked tired from exhaustion as most of them had a job to stand.

Dismounting from their horses Ixor with his Knights walked across the castle yard to the main building, on entering through the door at the top of the steps they met no resistance from any of the servants or squires, only now these subjects were bowing to Ixor as he passed them down this long corridor towards the great hall.

On entering the great hall the King was nowhere to be seen until Sir Endevoure grabbed a trembling servant by the arm. "Where is your King? Take us to him now."

This servant replied who at this time was at the point of collapsing. "Sir he has retired to his bed chamber, he has been there since he was seriously wounded in the arm from an arrow fired by one of your archers. If you care to follow me I shall take you to him."

As this servant knocked on the door of the chamber a maid appeared and immediately bowed to Ixor before letting him in with his entourage of Knights only to find a servant nursing the King who looked as though he was dying in his bed.

It was then that this servant said to Ixor. "Sir the King would like to talk to you and Sir Endevoure alone."

After the other Knights had left this chamber King Hobart beckoned Ixor and Sir Endevoure to come closer to his bedside, whispering to them in a frail condition the King said. "I never wanted it to come to this but you pushed me into a situation I could not escape from, only now I would like you Sir Endevoure to be a witness to my last will and testament."

Then with some effort this King handed a parchment to our Knight and asked him to read it out loud in front of Ixor.

Unrolling this parchment Sir Endevoure started to read this will, word for word. "I King Hobart Victinours hereby bequest the throne, its castle of Tonest with all its lands and buildings surrounding it to my nephew Ixor Victinours in the hope that he will become a true and just King.

Sir Endevoure had just finished reading this will when the Kings breathing started to falter just before he held his quill in his hand in ready for signing he said. "Now bring it to me to sign?"

Then with his hand shaking the King scribbled his signature upon this parchment before his shallow breathing started to quieten from which he suddenly passed away and died from the fever of his septic and painful wound.

That night there was silence within this castle for the men who had lost their lives from both sides as most of the survivors knew that the next day would be a day of clearing up the unsightly mess of bodies now scattered in and around the outside of these castle grounds.

Sure enough the very next morning the bodies of the dead were taken to a mass grave well away from the castle but not the late Kings body that was buried on a hill to the rear of the castle.

After these funerals of the fallen, Sir Endevoure was instructed from the other Knights to crown his stepson Ixor as the new King.

With most of his army of warriors watching from the ramparts, Ixor sitting on his throne in the middle of the castle yard now received the crown to his head from Sir Endevoure while saying these words. "I being a true Knight of the lands of Tonest crown Ixor Victinours our son of the Dragon Red to be our rightful King."

No sooner had he been crowned that there was a loud cheer from all his warriors along with the words. "Long live the King!" Long live the King!" Long live the King."

Chapter Thirty Six

A Score to be settled

Now that the rightful heir to the throne was settled, Sir Endevoure was longing to be back at the garrison with his wife Lady Silvianda but before this journey could be undertaken there was a lot of organization to be done getting the castle back to the way it was, so two days later after a discussion with King Ixor it was decided that Sir Endevoure along with the new King and half of his warriors were to travel back to the garrison while the other half of his men and most of the Knights stayed on at the castle.

On their return to the garrison its streets were alive with cheering people as this force of men paraded towards the manor house where on their arrival Lord Darnley was standing outside the front of this building with Lady Silvianda and princess Collesta.

As this parade of men eventually came to a halt, Sir Endevoure gave the command for them to disband as part of an order for them to return to their families.

After that morning's eventful reunion Sir Endevoure settled down for the next two weeks of socialising between his wife and whatever Lord Darnley had to offer in the way of parties for celebrating his grandson's victory over the late King of Tonest.

That time at the garrison passed quickly as it was decided that the wedding between King Ixor and Princess Collesta was to be held back at the castle because after this wedding, castle Tonest would be this Kings official state residence.

On their return to the castle all was ready for the great day as servants; squires and maid's had all worked vigorously over the last few days to make sure this marriage would run smoothly.

When the day eventually arrived all manner of dignitaries had travelled to this great event including Princess Collesta's father King Plestoe who had arrived that morning from across the seas to give his daughters hand away in marriage.

Now amongst the other Knights directly behind the King, Sir Endevoure witnessed this union of his sovereign to this lovely princess who was now beautifully dressed in front of the holy man inside this castle's chapel.

That night a large feast was held in the great hall to celebrate this marriage to the delight of most of the guests sitting at the side tables as in the last few days of the battle they had hardly eaten and were now hungry for food.

During that evening Sir Favour who was the best man for his majesty stood up with his goblet and said a few words for this great event.

"Lords, Ladies and gentlemen can I have your attention as I would like to give a toast to their majesties on their wedding day." "To the

King and Queen of Tonest castle may they both live long and happy lives."

Sir Favour wanted to say more but after the other Knights interrupted him to take it in turn while standing to say their well wishes for their King he had to wait to carry on.

Finally after all these Knights had finished their praises to their King, Sir Favour was at last able to stand again for the rest of his speech which shook all the Knight's into silence as he had decided to put up his sword for good and retire spending the remainder of his life helping the sick.

After the shock of Sir Favour's news the King took the Knight outside away from his guests but after trying to persuade him to stay to no avail this King had let him go.

The next day Lord Darnley accompanied his daughter Lady Silvianda by coach with six warriors in tow on their trip back to the garrison but left Sir Endevoure in riding clothes with just a sword for protection to ride off for the day to visit his pet Bisthion, but not before telling his wife that he would meet her again as soon as he could back at the garrison.

It was good to see his pet again down in this canyon of Vorth as these visits were mostly peaceful, the only problem was the smell from his Bisthion's urine, but to this Knight, after several weeks with the stench of warfare, this smell was something he could deal with.

As usual his pet came stealthily over to him as a sign of wanting to play until on this particular day there seemed to be something different about this animals approach as it looked as though his Bisthion was actually stalking him with his massive horns pointing down towards our Knight for the kill.

The problem was for Sir Endevoure he had already dismounted from his horse earlier at the bottom of the track so there was no way of avoiding this confrontation of his now dangerous pet.

Taking his sword from his scabbard Sir Endevoure started to back away slowly so as not annoy this animal into a mad frenzy of attack which was a waste of time anyway because the Bisthion charged at such speed that our Knight had to dive to one side, narrowly missing one of its horns.

While Sir Endevoure was on the ground he happened to glance over at the caves and to his astonishment he noticed another Bisthion with its head appearing from out of the furthest cave, it was only then he realised that he was no longer welcomed down in this canyon and that he should run for his life' but before he could do that he had to distract his pet, so with his sword he threw it as hard as he could in the other direction, this did the trick for a little while until the Bisthion realised that our knight was running to his horse from which this angry animal did a u turn and started to come back at him.

It must have been an eternity for Sir Endevoure when he ran while dodging in a zigzag formation to avoid being tossed in the air from this adamant animal, but lucky for him was his horse also was spooked and decided to become disoriented and instead of running away was now coming straight at him so with an almighty leap from our Knight he managed to land onto the horses' saddle before pulling on the reigns to lift this animal into the air and over the approaching Bisthion's body.

On doing so the horns of the Bisthion caught the underside of his horse making the animal nay out in pain before its hoofs made contact with the ground again sending our Knight forward in his saddle with a jolt, as he sat back in the saddle he pulled on its reigns with a mighty tug to one side to veer the horse into the direction of the track.

It must have been sheer terror that encouraged this horse's gallop to gather speed as it outpaced this Bisthion's final and desperate bid to gore his adversaries, only to miss this poor horse's rump by inches as the animal finally cantered up the long narrow track to safety where Sir Endevoure leaned over to pull the gate from behind to close it.

As his horse collapsed on its four fetlocks to the ground from exhaustion, Sir Endevoure was thrown from his saddle to the edge of the canyon cliff where he happened to see his Bisthion snuggling up to its mate in a way of affection.

From this day's lucky escape our Knight knew he would never be able to come close to his Bisthion again as nature had taken over returning his pet to its roots of being wild.

After tending to his horse's wound, Sir Endevoure galloped towards the land owner's farm house where he was informed by him that the other Bisthion had turned up one day from out of nowhere and because this animal was annoying this land owner's livestock he decided with the help of other landsmen to coax this animal down into the canyon for its own safety.

With the knowledge that his pet had its own life to lead now, Sir Endevoure decided it was time to concentrate more on his marriage with Lady Silvianda as he departed while leaving these lands of Vorst to their own devices.

Our Knight was soon back in familiar territory while riding through the forest just before the clearing to the garrison, with the warmth of the sun on his back was enough to make him feel at peace with himself this day from all those years of turmoil, little did he know was this peace was going to be short lived for him when his horse suddenly reared up from a taut rope springing from the ground in front of them.

Sir Endevoure's first reaction was to go for his sword, only on doing so he found it was not there as he had thrown it to distract his Bisthion, now with no sword our Knight was an easy target for these six barbarians who suddenly rushed out of the bushes carrying wooden lances, as they thrust their lances at our Knight he was immediately knocked from his horse where he managed to rise to his feet before receiving countless blows to his head and body.

Bruised and bleeding Sir Endevoure collapsed to the ground again.

Now laying down helpless these blows kept on coming until he passed out from concussion, even though our Knight was out for the count two of these men were still not satisfied as they made sure he stayed there by kicking Sir Endevoure several times in his groin and in his face.

Once these barbarians were satisfied that our Knight was not going to go anywhere they stripped him of all his clothes and then took his horse before throwing his body into the undergrowth and leaving him there naked to the elements.

With successfully committing this crime the barbarians led our Knight's horse to a small clearing some distance away to butcher this animal for food as their hunger in the last week had got the better of them.

It was when all six of them sat in front of their fire watching the roasting horse turning on its spit a Knight suddenly appeared from out of the heavy undergrowth amongst the bushes who just happened to be Sir Bellingham carrying a bag of coins in one hand and his sword in the other.

On seeing the Knight one of the men stood up to greet him before this Knight said to him. "Has the deed been done, is Sir Endevoure dead?"

"Yes my lord we made sure before we hid his body in the grass." This man replied while taking the coinage from Sir Bellingham before being warned by this Knight who still had his sword at the ready in case of trouble.

"Good now after today if I see any of you in these lands again I shall not be responsible for what happens to any of you, so enjoy your food and when you are finished just disappear, do you understand.

"Yes sir understood." This man replied as he sat down with his friends again.

Leaving these happy barbarians to share their coins out amongst themselves, Sir Bellingham disappeared into the trees but not too far as he had camped in amongst these trees with twenty of the castle's archer's only a short distance from these murderous curs.

On arriving back to his head archer Sir Bellingham said. "Place your men out of sight around the perimeter of these barbarian's camp then tell them to wait for my signal from a burning arrow then let them have hell."

"Yes Sir this should not take long my archer's never miss."

"Just make sure they don't or the King will not be very happy."

Now with his archer's in place, Sir Bellingham waited for the Barbarian's to finish stuffing themselves, when he was satisfied that they had eaten their fill this Knight pulled back his bow and let his flare go.

As soon as this arrow lit up the sky, twenty arrows flew thick and fast into the barbarian's camp with accurate result of every single shaft hitting the flesh of a barbarian killing them instantly on the spot.

Before the archers left that day, Sir Bellingham told them to retrieve their arrows but to leave these men where they lay for the crows.

When Sir Bellingham returned to the castle he reported straight back to King Ixor who was sitting alone in his great hall or so he thought if it was not for one of Queen Collesta's maids ear wigging from behind the kitchen's door at the far end of this hall.

"Well Sir Knight did you do what I asked of you?" The King inquired while pouring a goblet of wine for himself and Sir Bellingham.

"Yes Sire your step father Sir Endevoure is dead." Sir Bellingham replied as he lifted his goblet of wine as a toast.

"Did you make sure that there's no evidence of it coming back here to spite us?"

"Yes your majesty everything has been taken care of."

"Good once you have drunk your wine you can take your leave."

As Sir Bellingham left this hall the maid behind the door found her way back to Queen Collesta, on entering her mistress's chamber she reported to her all that she had overheard, only to be told by the queen to keep it as a secret and not to tell anyone else.

Later that evening while eating their evening meal Queen Collesta approached her husband the King and demanded to know why he had Sir Endevoure executed.

King Ixor was not happy that his wife had found out from one of her maids but decided to tell his wife the truth anyway of why he commanded it to happen.

"You cannot have someone going around killing royalty, that man killed my father all those years ago on the orders from my departed uncle the last King. You never know I might have been the next one that he would have killed, so I do not want to hear any more talk about the subject is that understood?"

"Yes my Lord I understand."

Queen Collesta then realised that her husband had used Sir Endevoure over the last few years for his own devices in order to become the King, once he had achieved that aim he had then taken his long awaited revenge on that Knight by having him killed.

Some time the next day the maid who had overheard the King talking was taken away by the Kings guards and was never seen again.

It must have been more than four days later that Sir Endevoure's decomposed body was found by roaming gypsies, who were travelling through the forest, after finding the other six rotting corpses that were laying around a half eaten horse on a spit over a dowsed fire somewhere near to where our Knight was killed.

Not recognizing who this naked man was these gypsies buried our Knight with the other six men in a hidden grave site amongst the undergrowth.

Back at the garrison Lord Darnley told his daughter that Sir Endevoure must be dead as he had not returned for some time to the garrison even though search parties had been sent out in the last few days to find him with no results.

As days turned into weeks, then months with Lady Endevoure now on her own, she retired to a spinster's life. In her heart, she hoped that one day she might see Sir Endevoure come riding up to the manor in his armour again as the BLACK KNIGHT.

THE END